A NOT
SO RUSTIC
RETREAT

HOLT JACOBS MYSTERY - BOOK 2

LILY STIRLING

~ To The Hardy Boys ~
Frank & Joe, thanks for all the adventures.

CONTENTS

CHAPTER 1

*N*o other options. No other options. Literally no other options.

Spending the Fourth of July in the mountains of Idaho wasn't my idea. First off, it's Idaho. *Idaho.* A far cry from my home in Seattle, Washington.

Do you know what Idaho's famous for? Potatoes. Do you know what Washington's famous for? Starbucks. That's right. Washingtonians created Starbucks while Idahoans were too busy digging in the dirt.

Maybe getting up at 4:00 a.m. and driving all morning had left me extra cynical, but I really wasn't prepared for my first glimpse of the little slice of heaven I was renting.

I'd been driving past lots of cabins that varied from calendar ready to decidedly ramshackle. But my GPS didn't drop me off at a normal cabin. No, I was delivered to a structure that was so high-concept modern that it was tacky. The place jutted into the sky in random geometric angles, gleaming gold with glass glinting in the sunshine.

Was that my house?

Maybe I should have glanced at the photos when I'd made the email reservation. But I'd been desperate, and with a name like The Hive, I'd assumed it would be an overly cutesy attempt at rustic. Small beds crammed into even smaller bedrooms. What I got was a millionaire's passion project that vaguely resembled a boxy beehive. After spending six hours in a car, it wasn't the welcome I'd expected.

A strange scent hit me as I got out of my car. I was surrounded by pine trees and Lake Coeur d'Alene.

Was that the smell of nature? Interesting. An actual forest smells way different from the evergreen car fresheners.

Ignoring my luggage, I grabbed the bags of groceries I'd picked up from Baycliff Grocery—the closest town's only grocery store. Ideally, I'd have started with a quick shower since I was rumpled in a way that happened only after hours in a car. But I was running out of time and had to begin making lunch.

Pressing in The Hive's four-digit code, I was prepared for an interior as ultramodern chic as the outside. I wasn't expecting a midsize dog growling inside the door.

Was this the wrong house?

My code had worked...or the door had already been unlocked. But that dog didn't belong to anyone I knew. "Hello?" I called, not sure what my next move should be. Then my baby sister, Juniper, appeared.

"Holt? You're here," she said, kneeling down to nuzzle the dog. My sister had the annoying habit of always looking perfect, and the solemn dog with the reddish mane only added to the idyllic picture that was Juniper.

Entering The Hive, I frowned. "What are you doing here?"

She tilted her head. "You invited me."

"I told you three p.m."

She laughed. "You said that. But then you forwarded the reservation info, which said we could arrive at eleven." Juniper popped her hip. "Jude and I thought you couldn't read."

I rolled my eyes. The possibility I might want some privacy was clearly too strange to be considered.

The dog barked.

"And what is that?" The trip had just started, and already I had a stress headache.

"A dog," Juniper said, in no mood to be helpful.

"The rental didn't come with a dog."

Juniper batted her eyes like a toddler trying to get out of trouble. "I brought him. Now I have two men in my life."

Squeezing my eyes shut, I set down the grocery bags and began rubbing my temples.

Juniper laughed. "Would you relax? The rental says pet friendly."

My eyes flew open. "You don't even own a dog!"

"I know." She let out an exasperated breath. "You asked me to come on this trip last minute. I'd already committed to watching him while his owners were on the East Coast. What was I supposed to do? Leave him at my place?"

"And a simple text saying, *FYI, Holt, I'm bringing a pet* was too much work?"

"Well, you never bothered telling me why you were taking a spontaneous vacation. And at least I asked about that."

Why I decided to take a sudden vacation was none of Juniper's business. So far, my biggest regret was inviting other people to come along.

I hadn't wanted to come across as a friendless hermit staying in an empty three-bedroom. But really, was the hermit route so bad?

When I didn't answer, Juniper shrugged. "That's what I thought. By the way, Jude and I took the master bedroom. We're the only couple here. Besides, you wouldn't believe how much luggage Chouzie has."

Chouzie? The dog's name was Chouzie?

"What kind of a name is Chouzie?"

"Holt, it's *Chouzie the Chow Chow*."

The way she gave the title, she clearly expected it to mean something to me. It didn't.

"Do you follow Chouzie? A lot of people follow Chouzie." Juniper began petting the dog. "Actually, Chouzie has more followers than I do. We're doing some cross-promotion, which should do wonders for my online presence."

I sighed. Having my sister make her living as a social media influencer definitely had its downsides.

"Now all we need is something to create a buzz to really solidify me with Chouzie's viewers," Juniper said. "I had something set up, but joining you in Idaho ruined it. Let me know if you have any ideas."

"I'll do that," I muttered.

I was still standing in the entryway beside my grocery bags. This wasn't working. For starters, I needed to put the milk in the fridge, then take stock of the kitchen and begin prep. There wasn't much time before lunch.

Ignoring the painfully modern furniture and tacky art, I picked up my bags and marched past my sister and her borrowed dog.

Wait. Had Juniper said she'd taken the master bedroom? Checking my phone, I saw there really wasn't time to squabble over room assignments. I could shove her luggage out of *my* master bedroom later.

Tossing stuff in the fridge, I began rifling through the cabinets, hunting for a mixing bowl. The kitchen looked fancy. Keyword being *looked*. In reality, everything seemed more like props for a show kitchen than usable tools.

When I finished my cabinet exploration, Juniper was perched on the kitchen island. "You know, this is how I imagine your apartment," she said.

"Very funny," I said, then realized she hadn't been kidding. "Seriously?" I tugged at my hair. "This is nothing like my place. First off, I have something called taste."

She raised her eyebrows like I was the difficult one. "I wouldn't know since I've never been invited."

"Um." I frowned. "You don't live in Seattle."

Juniper tossed her hair. "But I like adventures."

"Fine." I sighed, already on the hunt for a cheese grater. "You and Jude are welcome to visit me in Seattle."

She straightened on her perch. "Thank you."

"Wait, where is your husband?" I twisted around the kitchen like he was hiding in the pantry. "I didn't see your car."

"He drove to town to pick up a few things."

I nodded and began grating Parmesan. Somehow I needed to get her out of the cabin without making her suspicious. Unfortunately, Juniper's an extremely suspicious person. Did *Are you meeting him for lunch* sound casual enough?

"What are you smiling about?" Juniper asked.

"I'm not smiling."

There's a chance I was smiling. My jaw was sore from how much I'd grinned during the six-hour drive. But I shouldn't be smiling. A dog was party crashing, Juniper felt entitled to the master bedroom, and the trip was costing a small fortune.

"Mm-hmm." Juniper tapped a manicured finger to her lips. "The only time I saw you this goofy looking was when...No! Holt Jacobs, is she here? That ambulance lady?"

"Mind your own business." I tried to sound irritated, but there was no hiding my grin from the mention of my EMT, Brittany Asato.

"Ah!" Suddenly Juniper's arms were wrapped around me, and she was jumping. "Is she staying here? Are you two dating? When did this happen? Is that why you're in Idaho? I kept wondering since you hate Idaho..."

Freeing myself from Juniper's hold, I began mixing ingredients in a bowl while Juniper rapid-fired questions, never waiting for an answer.

Juniper and I met Britt two months ago during a mandatory family vacation my mom had planned in an over-the-top tourist town in Oregon. Juniper's interactions with Brittany were minimal. I, on the other hand, had a much greater need for first responder services—there were even scars to prove it. But, in the end, it was worth it. While solving a few crimes may have been some people's highlight, for me (as cringy as it sounds), the best part was hanging out with Britt.

"Holt!"

"Hm?"

"Is that why you're making lunch?" Juniper was quivering with excitement.

"Yup."

"Ah!"

If I gave Juniper an inch of encouragement, she'd be tackle-hugging me. So I remained unresponsive, creating scoops of gnudi and setting them on a waiting cookie sheet.

"All right." Juniper had shifted into planner mode. "I'll take Chouzie for a walk and meet up with Jude. Let me run upstairs and grab Chouzie's leash, and then we'll be out of your hair." With that, Juniper evacuated the kitchen.

At least Juniper was leaving without an argument. The only other person I'd invited was my buddy Darren. Hopefully, he'd follow the 3:00 p.m. arrival time.

Darren and I had met working at the same company. He'd coached me when I had to testify about an engineering patent. Afterward we became gym buddies and occasional lunchtime companions. If that's not the definition of BFFs, I don't know what is.

"Anyone home?" Darren called.

"Yeah," I answered. Could today get any worse?

"Why'd you tell us to come at three?" he asked, charging into the kitchen with two suitcases and a backpack.

I should've known a lawyer would read the fine print.

"Good to see you," I lied, abandoning lunch preparations for a quick bro hug. Then, checking my phone, I said, "Now drop off your stuff and leave. I have plans."

"Plans?" Darren tilted his head. "What kind of plans?"

Instead of answering, I smirked and put my pan of gnudi in the fridge to chill.

"Wait a second." He took in the kitchen. "Did you plan this whole trip because of a girl?"

"Go to your room."

"Your plans are a lunch date?" Darren's eyes grew big. "You rented a cabin in the woods for a lunch date?"

"Not just lunch."

"Wait. So you do have a lunch date?"

"Darren, no, that's not...What I meant was...go to your room."

"Okay, *Mom*." Darren headed for the stairs with his luggage and met my sister on her way down. Juniper was carrying the dog. It was huge in her arms, but its legs were short enough that it probably couldn't do the stairs. She set Chouzie down and eyed Darren curiously.

Instead of introducing himself to my sister, Darren's eyebrows creased. "Is that...? Is that Chouzie the Chow Chow?"

"Yes!" Juniper did a little twirl.

"Wow," Darren said.

I squeezed my eyes shut. She really didn't need encouragement.

"I'm Holt's little sister Juniper," she said.

Darren tore his eyes away from Chouzie to look at Juniper. "Darren," he said, extending his hand for a shake, but my sister hugged him instead.

Next, Juniper batted her eyes innocently as she said, "I didn't know Holt had any friends."

"Not many," Darren said, laughing. "And he doesn't exactly overshare. I just found out he planned this entire trip for a girl."

"I know." Juniper began bouncing on her toes. "It's so romantic."

I groaned. There's nothing romantic about wanting to be in the same location at the same time as someone else. It's practical.

I was halfway through chopping an onion before Juniper and Darren finished swapping the little information they had. You'd think they'd known each other for years. Inviting them had definitely been a mistake.

Once Darren headed upstairs, Juniper was pointing a finger at me. "Why didn't you warn me?"

I frowned. "I told you my buddy Darren was coming."

"Holt, you didn't say he was tall, dark, and gorgeous!"

I shot my sister a glare. "And you're married."

"He's so tall!"

I frowned. "We're the same height."

"Did you see his biceps?"

"I'm aware Darren has a lot of upper-body strength. But, to be clear," I said, looking up from my onions, "we work out the same amount. He just targets the upper body, while I do full-body workouts."

Juniper rolled her eyes. "Right. Sure."

Raising an eyebrow, I tilted my head toward the front door. "Don't you have somewhere to be?"

"Fine, I'm going." Juniper tossed her hair and made a melodramatic exit with Chouzie.

A couple of minutes later, Darren popped his head into the kitchen. "Did you know there's no toilet paper, only bidets in the bathrooms?"

For the record, I hadn't known. But Brittany was expected any minute, and it wasn't the time. When I pointed to the door with my knife, Darren took the hint and left.

My eyes had begun stinging from the onions when I heard voices out front.

Please, no.

But of course. Why would the day go how I wanted? There was Darren chatting with Brittany. Why wouldn't they bump into each other on his way out? Abandoning the marinara sauce I had started heating on the stove, I charged outside.

"Exactly, Oregon is great," Darren was saying with the grin he used when trying overly hard to be charming.

"Brittany, hi." I didn't overthink hugging her. Or I only overthought it after my arms were wrapped around her. Thankfully, she hugged me back.

It was a perfect opportunity to shoot Darren a death glare. He shrugged, his smile never slipping...My death glare works best with strangers. Then surprise flashed across his face. "Are you crying?" he asked.

Britt's eyes turned professional as she moved back and took in my face.

I sighed. This wasn't a sexy start.

"Not crying," I said. "I've been cutting onions for lunch."

"Right." But Darren didn't sound convinced. Then, instead of leaving, he asked another question. "So, Brittany, where are you staying?"

I would kill him. Darren was a dead man.

"A short walk up the road." Britt's eyes danced, sensing my agony.

"Really now?" Darren tilted his head while he decided what question to ask next. "Holt lives in Seattle. You live in Oregon. How did you end up on the same vacation? Did you meet online?"

Some people shut down under Darren's questions—though that's usually in the courtroom. Brittany showed no signs of being intimidated. Her smile was almost lazy as she said, "Holt's here because I invited him." She let that sink in for a moment before adding, "His vacation at Amelia's Haven wasn't very relaxing. My trip was already planned, and since we both like the woods, I thought this would be a perfect spot for him."

Darren shot me a glance that asked, *You like the woods?*

"Well, now that's done with..." I offered Britt my arm. I wasn't being chivalrous. I needed to drag her away from Darren. My friend wasn't leaving, and Brittany was too polite to walk away.

Darren pretended to be offended. "Wait. We just got introduced."

"Darren," I growled.

He laughed. "All right. All right. I'm going."

"Nice to meet you," Britt called as I tugged both of us into The Hive. We'd made it to the entryway when she asked, "What is that?"

"My friend when I'm not plotting his demise," I grumbled.

"How often do you plot his demise?"

"Depends on how often I see him."

Britt's lips quirked as she tried not to laugh. "Good to know. But actually I was asking about that." She was pointing to the entryway wall, where a waterfall of mirrored globes cascaded down to the floor.

Taking a moment to smooth back my hair, I said, "Modern chic artwork."

"Ah. It's...impressive."

I frowned. Did she also think it was my taste? I literally had no choice in what my rental looked like. "You do realize this isn't my artwork?"

Brittany gave a light laugh. "Right."

We made it to the kitchen, and I stirred the sauce. I'd volunteered to cook lunch because the meals I'd seen Brittany eat via webcam relied heavily on the freezer section. But, to be honest, I had no idea what I was doing. This was uncharted territory. In the past, the most I'd done for a relationship was run a 10K. And, technically, Brittany and I weren't even dating. We'd been doing the weird dance of frequent texts and video calls. Not dating, but not *not* dating. So what had compelled me to drop everything and go to Idaho, of all places?

"You good?" Britt asked, putting her hand on my arm. Her deep brown eyes caught more than I wanted.

"Yeah, uh, yeah. It's good to see you," I managed.

When I looked down at her hand, a bit of tension left my shoulders. She wasn't wearing an engagement ring.

Oh, have I mentioned her dead fiancé? Kind of a big deal and part of the whole debacle I'd helped clear up. Anyway, though it had been around two years since her fiancé's murder, she'd still worn the ring in May.

Am I a bad person for being glad it was gone?

Clearing my throat, I moved to the cutting board. "Once I finish chopping the onions, they'll be sautéed and added to the marinara. The gnudi is chilling in the fridge. Pretty soon, it'll be ready to boil."

A tiny scar by Britt's right eyebrow became more apparent. Had I messed up already? "So most of the cooking is already done? How will I know you made it?"

Was that the problem? My chest expanded. "You could take my word for it."

Britt took a step closer. "What if that's not good enough?"

"I had witnesses! Darren and Juniper both saw me cooking."

She took another step closer. "Friends and family never lie?"

Oh. Brittany was flirting. Heat rose up my face. I should have caught on sooner. "Are you saying in the future I'll need to cook you another meal from start to finish?"

Brittany pursed her lips, seeming to think it over. "Yeah, that should work."

That's when I should have kissed her. Right then. But I chickened out. The most we'd ever done was hold hands, and since I'd been on a gurney at the time, it doesn't really count.

Blinking away some onion tears, I finished chopping and was quickly distracted by my frying pan options. The Hive was advertised as being *fully stocked*, but the one frying pan they had *in stock* was whack, and the spatulas were a cheap plastic that could easily snap in half. I was in a perfect-looking kitchen with cheap props that might melt on a burner.

How was I supposed to cook with such a cheap pan? My jaw tightened. I was an adult. I could let it go. It wasn't a big deal. Sure, I'd have packed up my kitchen's cooking supplies if I'd known. But it was fine.

Stay calm. It's not a big deal. Don't start ranting.

How would Britt feel about an impromptu shopping trip? She was watching me with that amused look on her face.

"Those onions sure make your eyes water," she commented.

I decided against the shopping trip.

Taking a deep breath, I tried to smile. "Yup. It's definitely the onions. Not the cooking equipment that was stolen from a kid's playhouse."

Brittany struggled to remain serious. "But you're a good enough cook to work with what you have. Right?"

I took the bait. "Mm-hmm. I'm that good."

Beginning to sauté the onions, I prayed I didn't snap the spatula in two. With Britt right there, I kept further complaints about the equipment to myself—though I couldn't help a couple of groans escaping during the cooking nightmare.

I was just beginning to relax when scuffling sounds started by the back door. Was Juniper back with her borrowed dog? She knew better than to come back early...right? The back door neighbored the kitchen and dining room. Sliding past Brittany, I was prepared to face this newest intruder armed with a flimsy spatula.

CHAPTER 2

When the door finally opened, I was face-to-face with a crooked-nosed stranger wearing medical gloves. We both hesitated. There were two men behind him, and one of them didn't need to recover.

"Keep your head down!" he ordered. "Get back. Get back. We're coming in."

The first clue should have been the medical gloves. The neon orange neck gaiters they were pulling above their noses was another hint they weren't dropping off a pie. I only saw the first thug's face before they were all covered. The second thug had a hoodie pulled over his forehead, while the guy giving the orders had a bear tattoo on his forearm.

Could I warn Britt without them knowing she was here? She could sneak out the front door. Mr. Bear Tattoo was so focused on me, he hadn't checked the kitchen. I was trying to figure out how to alert Brittany when she rounded the corner. Her surprise was quickly replaced by her professional paramedic mask.

"Can I help you?" Her voice was pleasant with an undercurrent of steel I'd never heard before.

"Both of you lie down on the ground and don't move. It'll all be over soon."

I reached out and took Brittany's hand as we tugged each other to the floor.

"Keep your heads down," Mr. Bear ordered.

I stared down at the textured laminate of the fake wood floor, one hand gripping Brittany's, the other still holding the spatula. That thing was barely a match for onions and would be useless against burglars.

Mr. Bear stood guard over us while the footsteps of his two thugs echoed up the stairs. Slams from doors and closets drifted down, mixed with other sounds of destruction.

What was happening?

This was so messed up. Also, I would have handled being a hostage with so much more class and grace if not for my lunch. The marinara was on low heat, but my poor onions didn't stand a chance. Sizzling turned into strangled popping sounds as the pan ran out of oil, and the smell of burning onions began drifting through the air.

I shifted on the floor. Forgotten was the chaos going on upstairs. Instead, I was experiencing physical pain at what was happening to my innocent onions. All they'd wanted was to fulfill their destiny and be successfully sautéed for my lunch. Instead, they were being ruthlessly burned while I lay powerless on the floor.

When gray smoke started floating through the air, I couldn't take it anymore. "Please," I said, twisting a little toward my captor.

"Head down," Mr. Bear ordered.

Right.

I tried again with my lips practically kissing the floor. "Please, just turn the burner off."

Brittany's hand tightened in mine.

"So you have time to run away?" he asked.

I groaned. "No. So they'll stop burning."

Brittany turned her head toward me and murmured, "Isn't it wrecking the pan?"

I rolled my eyes, and Britt giggled—she'd giggled in the middle of a home invasion.

My romantic date with Brittany hadn't been ideal before the breaking and entering. Still, burned food was something I'd promised wouldn't happen.

If I squeezed my eyes shut hard enough, could I wake myself up? This had to be a nightmare.

Sensing my distress, Britt raised her head and said, "The smoke detector will go off if you don't fix the burner."

The guy behind us didn't respond. When I dared a peek, the flex of his jaw was obvious even through the mask. Were we more annoying than his usual hostages?

Britt squeezed my hand before saying, "Most vacation rentals are wired to call the fire department when the smoke detector goes off. They don't want tourists burning down houses."

I glanced at Brittany. Was that true?

When Mr. Bear didn't make a move, Brittany asked, "Is that what you want? A bunch of emergency personnel driving up?"

The guy shifted from one foot to another before yelling upstairs. Thug #1 came down and shut off the burner.

Thank you, I mouthed.

Brittany winked, and we both returned to staring at the floor.

In movies, during hostage situations, there's always some idiot who tries to be a hero and gets everyone in trouble. What movies don't show is how powerless and slimy it feels to just wait it out.

Were the intruders even armed? The first guy had been as surprised to see me as I was to see him. They wore gloves but covered their faces only when they saw The Hive wasn't empty. When I shifted to size up Mr. Bear, he yelled at me to stay still.

Fantastic.

The last time Brittany and I were in the same place, I'd had one mishap after another. This was supposed to be different. This vacation was far from Amelia's Haven and my mother. What could go wrong?

So far, the only difference was a pan of burned onions.

The sounds of destruction around the house grew louder. I don't know what they expected to find, but whatever they wanted wasn't showing up.

Mr. Bear left his spot and called his two thugs for a hushed conversation by the stairway. The words were unintelligible, but one voice was defensive while the other two were frustrated.

We were so close to the back door. Could we make a run for it? Brittany's grip tightened, and she shook her head. Usually, her practicality was an asset. Deciding to trust her, I stayed put.

"Look harder," Mr. Bear barked at his thugs before returning to his post.

This was getting ridiculous. "I don't know what you want," I said, obediently keeping my head down. "We arrived this morning. You can have my wallet and keys. Other than that, all you'll find are swimsuits and sunglasses."

Then again, my sunglasses are pretty expensive.

The guy didn't bother responding. It was time to stay silent. Mouthing off to kidnappers has historically been a bad idea. Besides, it wasn't just me. I had Brittany to think about. I couldn't get her in trouble. So I should stay silent...right?

Britt's thumb began stroking my palm. Could she tell my heartbeat was spiking?

Thug #1, with the crooked nose, began tearing apart the kitchen, while Thug #2, in the hoodie, began removing couch cushions. "Should I cut it open?" he asked, holding a fuchsia throw pillow.

"No," Mr. Bear said, incredulous, like Thug #2's IQ was in the single digits.

Outside there was a bark. Had a vehicle approached? Then came Juniper's voice saying something about a kayak. My eyes darted to Brittany. It was one thing for my date to be accidentally held hostage. It was a whole other thing to knowingly let my baby sister walk into a trap. I don't know much about chow chows, but that fur bag she called a dog wasn't much of a menace.

Brittany let go of my hand, which I assumed was her blessing. I tried to roll up from my stomach and lunge at Mr. Bear with the agility of James Bond.

I'm not James Bond.

The guy was waiting for me. I was lunging forward on one foot when, for half a second, the bear tattooed on his forearm stared at me. Then his fist connected with my jaw, and I crumpled to the floor.

There was a buzzing in my ears as someone called, "Let's go."

I was struggling to my hands and knees when the screen door opened, and Juniper's grinning dog was all over me. Juniper entered, followed by Jude.

While my sister was busy talking about the best time to kayak, my brother-in-law surveyed the ransacked house and Britt and me on the floor. In a moment, he'd grabbed Juniper, shoved her back outside, shut and dead-bolted the door, before doing a somersault roll behind the sofa.

Was my brother-in-law James Bond?

Outside, Juniper knocked on the glass, demanding to be let in. Meanwhile, her dog had moved on from licking me to licking Brittany.

"How many?" a voice asked from behind the sofa.

"Three," I said.

"They just left out the back," Britt said.

Jude looked me straight in the eyes—the first time I'd seen his eyes. "Are you sure?"

We nodded.

Jude said something under his breath before running back to the front door. He undid the locks, then called in a low voice, "Juniper?"

When my sister didn't appear, Jude ran across the house to the back door and collided with Juniper as she let herself in.

"That's not funny!" she began. "This is supposed to be relaxing. How does locking your wife out of the cabin fit in?"

Jude pulled Juniper behind him and checked outside for signs of our intruders. Satisfied, he locked the back door and then grabbed Juniper, holding her tightly. My sister's threats and protests were muffled before stopping completely.

Finally, Jude pulled back. "I'm sorry," he said. "Bad people were here, and I needed to make sure you were safe." It wasn't much of a speech, but considering the last vacation he hadn't said five words, it was enough. Juniper started kissing him all over his face and neck.

"Gross," I said. Not that I blamed her. After Jude's spy moves, I was a little in love with the guy.

"Holt?" Brittany was standing over me with her hand outstretched. Why was I still on my hands and knees?

I took her hand, and she helped me up more than I would have liked. The little scar by her eyebrow was defined, but she smiled slightly. "I think you can drop your weapon now."

I followed her gaze to my other hand. Not only was I still clutching the spatula, but I was holding it out in front of me like a knife.

Placing the spatula on the ultramodern dining table, I pretended not to be embarrassed. Time to be the responsible engineer everyone knew I was. Clearing my throat, I said, "We should call the police."

"Yeah," Britt said.

I grabbed my phone and was dialing 911 when there was an incoming call from my mother. "Not now," I muttered.

Mom had an uncanny ability to know when I was in trouble. Hard to come across as capable to a date with my mommy asking if I'd eaten my vegetables. I could let it go to voicemail, but she would keep calling until she received proof of life. Besides, if I put her off too long, she'd try Juniper, and I didn't trust the version of events Juniper would give.

"One sec," I said to Britt. Moving to the living room, I answered. "Hey, Mom."

"Holt?" Mom managed to get so much meaning in one word.

I was an adult. I could communicate. "Hey, we're all fine at the rental. There was an...issue we are dealing with. I can't talk now."

Mom didn't reply immediately. When she did answer, her voice was quiet. "Are you all right?"

Running a hand along my sore jaw, I answered truthfully since she would know if I was lying. "Mostly."

Mom was saying something, but I got distracted by Juniper talking to Brittany in the dining room. I knew that face. My sister was not to be trusted. "Sorry, Mom. I really need to go."

"I love you," Mom said.

"You too," I said before ending the call and joining Britt and Juniper in the dining room as fast as possible.

Juniper was midsentence when I arrived. "...the ambulance lady Holt thought was a murderer."

Had she just said that?

"Oh." Brittany's eyes widened. "You thought I was a murderer?"

I can fix this. Say something smart.

"Um, well..." Then my mouth hung open and no sound came out. Words like *just the one time,* or *that was weeks ago* weren't appropriate answers.

"You didn't tell her?" Juniper asked, looking genuinely surprised.

"Have you called 911?" Jude asked.

911?

I looked from Jude, to Brittany, to Juniper.

Someone was getting murdered. The question was, would Brittany kill me, or would I kill Juniper?

"We haven't called 911," Brittany told Jude. "They left when you arrived."

Jude went to the kitchen and made the call. Brittany's eyes lingered on me, her face unreadable. Then she followed Jude to give details. Britt was used to emergencies, though granted she was usually on the other side of them.

I popped my jaw back and forth. The adrenaline was wearing off, and my face decided to remind me I'd taken a punch. Sighing, I sat on one of the dining chairs.

"You didn't tell your girlfriend you originally thought she was a murderer?" Juniper asked, totally unconcerned about the ransacked house, her husband calling the police, or the massive skeleton she'd pulled out of my closet.

Not up to having this conversation, I chose a different route. "Brittany isn't technically my girlfriend."

"Okayyy," Juniper said.

"Not officially. We haven't labeled anything."

"But you came for her. Right? That's why you're in Idaho?"

I shrugged. I'd had enough questions, and the police hadn't even arrived. "You know how much I love Idaho."

"Didn't you say that in Idaho, the only thing more rabid than the raccoons were the people?"

So, I don't remember saying that...but it does sound like something I might say. Seriously, who would willingly get stuck in the backwoods of Idaho? Unfortunately, I didn't choose where Brittany took her vacation. I could only tag along when invited.

Before Juniper could dig further, Jude and Brittany returned.

"The sheriff's coming," Brittany said.

Sheriff? What was this, the Wild West?

Chouzie was growling at the bottom of the stairs. "What is it, boy?" Juniper asked before picking him up and going up to investigate.

Before I had time to prepare, Brittany's hand was lightly touching my chin. Standing up, I gazed at her lips and wondered if we should kiss. Could I be forgiven so quickly? I was moving my hand to cup her cheek when she said, "Your jaw's already bruising."

"I'll get some ice," Jude said, practically running from the room.

Britt's hand was still on my jaw. "How does it feel?"

I was about to answer when Brittany began moving my jaw, feeling all the points. It was like when the dentist asked a question before shoving a hand into your mouth. I flinched when she reached a tender spot and shrugged when she apologized.

"I don't think there's any permanent damage," Brittany said. "We could take you to the hospital to double-check."

"Not necessary," I said, batting her hand away. I wasn't going to be as helpless in the aftermath as I'd been during the break-in.

How would I check on Britt?

Before I could figure it out, Juniper came downstairs with her borrowed dog right as Jude returned with a bag of ice. "Did you see what they did upstairs?" Juniper asked, finally showing interest in our little break-in.

We shook our heads.

Immediately Jude's stance changed to high alert. What was his job? My other brother-in-law did investing or accounting...something with math and computers. But had I ever heard about Jude?

Juniper's eyes lit up at the chance to deliver information. "Upstairs is trashed. They removed all the bedding and dumped out all the bags—even Chouzie's."

"If only you'd come at three," I said loud enough that everyone heard but quiet enough they could pretend not to.

Juniper rolled her eyes. "What were they expecting to find in a dog's luggage?"

I began massaging my temples. "I don't know. Does Chouzie have any diamond collars?"

"No. If anything, Chouzie could be held for ransom."

A strange look overtook her face, one I had a lifetime of reasons to distrust. She began pacing as Chouzie sat innocently on his dog bed. "Chouzie's insured. His owners live off his earnings. They even made me get a background check before I could watch him."

I squeezed my eyes shut, not liking where this was headed. What had Juniper said? She needed to *create buzz* to get viewers?

"I mean, one could argue there's a narrative that this break-in"—Juniper picked up one of the fuchsia throw pillows for emphasis—"was all one big dognapping attempt."

Wow. This was a time when I'd expected stupid and got something even dumber than imagined.

Juniper's face turned red when no one started applauding or bowing down before her magnificent theory. "It's plausible," she said.

"Right," I said.

How were we related? I get creating media buzz, but her idea was too absurd.

"Stop looking at me like that!" Juniper said. "Chouzie could be held for a very high ransom...or maybe an obsessed fan wanted him."

I glanced at Brittany. This trip was supposed to be different, yet here was an additional example highlighting my crazy family.

"If it helps," I told Brittany, "Juniper doesn't believe this botched dog-snatching story. She just needs to sell it for social media."

Juniper crossed her arms. "And what if I do believe my brilliant idea?"

I snorted and was punished with flames shooting up my jaw. "No way."

"You're accusing me of knowingly misleading my followers?"

I took a deep breath. This was going nowhere. "Didn't you say the bedding was removed?"

"Yes, but—"

"And what, they thought your fifty-pound dog was hiding between the sheets?"

Brittany's laugh caught our attention, while Jude was too busy on his phone to care. "I'm sorry," Britt said. "Please carry on."

Juniper ignored my question and began fussing with Chouzie's lion's mane. "It's a good thing we weren't here. Poor Chouzie would have been so traumatized if he'd been dognapped."

I raised an eyebrow. "What about my trauma?"

"Eh," Juniper said, tossing her hair.

"There's no way this was attempted dognapping, and you know it."

Had I said *dognapping*? Juniper was a bad influence.

"Holt," Juniper said, fixing her hair. "Can you prove this wasn't an attempt to capture poor Chouzie?"

"Yes! Everything about this proves it wasn't an attempt to nab your dog."

"He's not my dog," Juniper sang on her way upstairs with Chouzie.

"Don't move anything," I yelled. "The police are coming."

"It's the sheriff," she called back.

What's the difference?

CHAPTER 3

J uniper's voice drifted down the stairs, sounding extra energetic as she recorded her dognapping theory. She would milk this incident for all it was worth.

I sat back down and eased the ice onto my face. Britt sat beside me, her eyes holding professional concern. Was it a good thing she was ignoring the whole *suspected murderer* thing?

She was probably running down a mental checklist to see if I was exhibiting signs of shock. Looking her over, I tried to remember my own checklist from my college lifeguarding days. She wasn't trembling or sweating excessively. Did that mean she was fine?

"So, Holt," Brittany said.

"Yeah?"

"You throw up on first dates. Have break-ins during second dates. What happens on third dates?"

I raised an eyebrow. "You'll have to wait and see."

Instead of smiling, her face still held professional concern. "Okay" is all she said.

What did *okay* mean? Was it a professional *okay*? Like my reactions were *okay* considering the circumstances? Or was it because I'd talked about a third date and after today she never wanted to see me again?

Ugh. Britt had liked me enough to stay in touch after I left Oregon. But this? Every time Britt saw me, I needed the police or paramedics.

Resting my face against the ice in my hand, I said, "You're really around at the worst possible times. My life usually isn't..." I sighed and gestured around the chaos. "I promised a good meal, and all you got was burned onions."

Her mouth twitched, the first responder's mask almost slipping. "This was better than our first date."

She had to go there? I ran a self-conscious hand through my shortened hair. "Since you shaved my head last time, I guess it's an improvement."

"Well"—Brittany's eyes sparkled—"don't be too sure it won't happen again. The day's still young."

That caught me off guard, and I gave a surprised laugh.

Britt smiled. "I got you to laugh."

I tried to frown. "Don't get used to it."

There was a knock at the door. Britt and I both jumped—so she *was* shaken.

Jude walked past us to the door. "Sheriff's here," he said.

Too bad. I really needed to have a grown-up conversation about whether Britt was crazy enough to see what would happen on a third date.

A woman in uniform entered. She had a braid going down to her hips, and her face was prematurely wizened from cigarettes and sunshine. Plus, I'd be willing to bet she'd worked at a couple of bait shops in her life.

After introductions, the sheriff got straight to business.

"Was anything stolen?" she asked.

"Not that we know of," I said. "We didn't touch anything until you came."

"They all wore gloves," Britt added.

We started a walk-through of the house. My frying pan of burned onions and the pot of marinara blended into the mess of open cupboards and strewn groceries in the kitchen. Thug #1 had even moved the fridge away from the wall. I don't know what he thought was back there, but I'm positive he wasn't looking for a chow chow.

For the first time since entering The Hive, I went upstairs. Since I'd waited until after the break-in, I got an armed escort. The decor and general ambience weren't helped by the robbers. Tacky artwork and funky pillows littered the master bedroom, blending in with dumped-out suitcases. There wasn't much to wreck in the master bath, but for some reason they'd torn off the shower curtain.

Thankfully, Juniper had stopped recording by the time we entered. She'd told us about the bedding strewn across the floor but had neglected to mention the mattress and box springs flipped off the bed.

The sheriff knelt down and picked up one of Chouzie's chew toys. Chouzie growled. She replaced the toy. "Since they wore gloves, we don't need to dust for prints. I'll take a few pictures, and then you can clean up and see if anything's missing."

I expected her to get a fancy camera from her patrol car. Instead, she took her cell phone—a couple of generations too old—and snapped a few shots.

Was that *standard procedure* or *backwoods procedure*?

While The Local Sheriff was busy, I met Juniper's eyes before tilting my head toward Chouzie. It was sibling code for: *I dare you to share your dognapping theory with the sheriff.* Juniper rolled her eyes but stayed silent.

Since my luggage was still in the car, I was free to join Britt at the dining table with the sheriff to review the break-in details while Jude and Juniper took care of their bags.

It would be rude to say *I told you so*, but if they'd all come when I told them to, they wouldn't be in this mess.

The Local Sheriff was grim-faced yet almost bored as she began the interview. I couldn't imagine the drudgery of overseeing locals and vacationers in the middle of nowhere.

"Was the back door unlocked?" she asked.

I frowned. "I didn't open it. There were sounds. I think they used a code."

She nodded like it was what she'd expected. Was this a common problem?

"And this is a Camarata Property?"

"Uh, maybe," I said.

Britt's mouth quirked at my answer.

The sheriff gave a half nod. "The Hive is a Camarata Property." Her tone made it clear she knew it was an eyesore. Had there been a petition to keep it from being built?

"And when did you rent the property?" she continued.

I glanced at Brittany, worried by the direction the questions were going. "Two and a half weeks ago," I said, keeping my voice even.

The sheriff looked up from where she'd been writing, showing the first hint of interest. "This was available for the week of July Fourth, two and a half weeks ago?"

Would she believe it was so ugly no one wanted it, even during a major holiday? I squirmed in my chair, wishing Brittany wasn't sitting beside me. "Sort of," I said.

The sheriff's eyes narrowed. "What do you mean, sort of?"

I smoothed back my hair. "It took some finagling."

At this point, The Local Sheriff wasn't the only one who'd grown suspicious. That little scar by Brittany's eyebrow was visible, and her eyes were unreadable. Neither of them said anything. I'd gone from victim to suspect in seconds.

Trying not to look at Brittany, I gave a better explanation. "I contacted the rental agent and asked him to name his price to let me rent any cabin in the area. The trip was last-minute and everything was booked, but I really had to be here." I couldn't stop myself from glancing at Brittany. This would either be really romantic or extremely creepy. After today's break-in, the future of our almost relationship was already on questionable ground. Her face was unreadable, but she hadn't run from the room screaming.

"And how much did you pay?" The sheriff had grown curious.

"Enough," I said.

"I see." The world-weary look she gave us left the impression our sheriff had been a romantic once, and it left her jaded. Good thing I'm already jaded.

"Someone tried to take Chouzie?" Darren wasn't shy about announcing his arrival, even with a patrol car parked outside. He strode into the dining room and stood at the head of the table. "When I watched Juniper's update, I came right away."

My jaw ticked as The Local Sheriff asked, "What's Chouzie?"

"A dog." I shook my head. "I...My sister...She has a social media thing..."

"Chouzie's safe," Britt told Darren, her eyes sparkling.

Darren nodded. His face remained friendly, but his shoulders widened as he took in the trashed surroundings. He extended his hand to the sheriff. "Darren Woods."

She shook. "Sheriff Misty Collins."

When Darren didn't make any move to leave, I said, "You can head up and check your stuff. Juniper and Jude are up there and can give you more information." Would The Local Sheriff think I was overstepping?

"Sure thing." Darren's eyes lingered on my ice pack. "I can't take you anywhere," he said. Then Darren leaned close to Brittany and murmured, "Holt plans very exciting dates. I hope he's worth it." With that, Darren was gone.

Thankfully, both Britt and the sheriff were unaffected by his charm and The Local Sheriff continued the interview like he'd never appeared. "What time did the break-in start?"

A couple of questions later, Jude came down and reported nothing missing from their bags—shocking no one stole Chouzie's designer chew toys.

Jude began cleaning up the kitchen, while Juniper had yet to make an appearance. She must be explaining all her theories to Darren. Would he play along with her dognapping idea?

"Were they carrying any weapons?" the sheriff asked.

That was an excellent question. Between the neon masks and latex gloves, I hadn't looked for more reasons to do what they said.

Britt shrugged.

"We don't know," I said.

At that the sheriff underlined something in her notebook. Was a lack of weapons suspicious in Idaho?

The sheriff was wrapping up her questions when Darren reported nothing was missing. The sheriff nodded. She didn't seem surprised. Like at all. By anything. Our vacation home had been entered using a code with tourists inside. The house was ransacked with nothing taken, and the sheriff wasn't surprised by any of it.

There's a reason I hate Idaho.

I clenched my jaw shut to keep myself from saying something rude. The Local Sheriff explained she was going to her patrol car to look up some information and she might be back with more details. I gave a somewhat polite nod while the other adults took on the brunt of social obligations.

When she left, my jaw was numb and tingly from the ice, and it was way past lunchtime.

Ideally, that's when I would have grabbed a snack, dumped all my sister's luggage out of the master bedroom, and turned into a hermit. But I couldn't leave. In a strange way, I was still on a date. I'd promised lunch, and it was approaching supper. Also, Brittany, Juniper, and Darren were all staring at me.

Why was everyone worried about me? Brittany had gone through the same ordeal.

After making my way to the kitchen, I poured the bag of mostly melted ice down the sink. The trio of worried faces had followed, with Chouzie joining the parade. I tried to grin. "Who's hungry?"

Jude was moving around the kitchen. At first all I noticed was the clean pan. Jude had scraped the burned gunk completely off. Sure, it was still a cheap knockoff, but what Jude had accomplished was truly impressive. Then I saw the rest of the kitchen was also set to rights.

It wasn't until a timer went off that I noticed the boiling water. Jude had cooked my romantic meal for two. A bag of salad was opened, and the meal was shared between the five of us. Darren was right. I did plan exciting dates.

We began eating. With Darren and Juniper at the table, conversation flowed around me. I just wanted to lie down. I'd been around so many people today. And not just people but *talking people*. It was all so exhausting.

But I needed to figure things out with Brittany. Still, that couldn't happen with Darren or Juniper around.

Juniper elbowed me. "Are you paying attention?" she asked.

"Yeah."

"Sure you are." Juniper rolled her eyes. "As I was saying, according to this article, Camarata Properties has been in business for thirty-plus years. They own rentals in multiple states, and their main income is university housing."

"Wow. Truly fascinating stuff, sis."

Juniper ignored me. "The Hive was a pet project for Mr. Camarata's second wife." Juniper wrinkled her nose as she skimmed the article. "Oh. His daughter is getting married in a couple of weeks in their vacation home off Lake Coeur d'Alene."

I leaned back in my chair. Was Juniper stressed? Since when did she read bios as dinner conversation? "Does it list a local office?"

"Uh, hold on." After a few taps on the screen, Juniper said, "Yes, Camarata Properties has an office in Baycliff."

"When does it close?"

"Five."

It was 5:03 p.m. And the day's streak of perfect timing just got better. "Tomorrow, then," I said, bringing my plate to the kitchen.

"Tomorrow?" Darren asked the question, but everyone else was watching.

I frowned. Wasn't it obvious? "Someone used a code to get in here. I'd like to ask the Camaratas how that happened."

"What if the Camaratas aren't in the office?" Brittany asked.

I couldn't tell if she was serious. Reminding myself to stay calm, I said, "Then I'll talk to the property manager."

Juniper giggled. "Holt's mad."

"I'm not mad!"

Okay, so I may have been irritated. Give me a break. I'd driven six hours, fasted, been a hostage, and had a police interview. Not exactly a good day.

Before things could escalate, The Local Sheriff returned with a tablet open to pictures of bear tattoos from people who'd been arrested. I looked through all of them, but none were a match. I'd just vetoed the final bear tattoo when a stranger opened the screen door and called for Brittany.

Chouzie gave a warning growl, his lion's mane helping his fierceness.

"I'm here, Sienna," Britt said, leaving the table to greet this newest intruder.

The woman who entered may have been Juniper's age. She had a real Mother Earth vibe. Her clothes were in earthy tones and probably organic. At any rate, they looked unbelievably soft. She was really short and actually pulled off dreadlocks.

To recap, Brittany was really cool. She had a friend who was really cool. Then there was me, who got punched in the face and was ready to curl into the fetal position after being around too many people.

"What happened?" Britt's friend asked—had Brittany called her Sierra? The question was directed at Brittany, but her eyes darted between Jude, Darren, and me, trying to figure out who Britt's troublemaker was.

"Oh, you know," Brittany hedged. "Just a little confusion about who was renting the cabin."

The friend's eyes lingered on The Local Sheriff. "Right," she said. "Well, you've been gone a while, and when I saw the cop car out front, I thought I'd check."

How did she know where my rental was?

As if reading my thoughts, Brittany flushed. "I told them where I was going, just in case..."

"I was a kidnapper?" I finished.

Brittany bit her lip and gave a slight nod. Was she embarrassed?

"Phew," I said. "That should make us even for that whole *suspecting you of murder thing.*"

Brittany's lips quivered, but she restrained a smile. "That was weeks ago."

The sheriff cleared her throat, more uncomfortable with the flirting than the criminal accusations. "I'll be in touch," she said and headed out the door.

The dreadlock friend began talking the moment the sheriff left. "You'll want to work on your story. You were gone so long, your mom was threatening to come down here and check on you. So I hid her shoes and ran for the door. If she sees the sheriff...Well, prepare yourself."

Brittany nodded, her face turning impassive. "Thanks," she said. "Give me a minute, and I'll walk up with you."

Mrs. Asato was also at their cabin? I swallowed. Given the circumstances, that was not great. Though are there ever good circumstances for meeting an almost girlfriend's parents? I'd met Britt's twin brother, Paul, in May, but there had never been a reason to meet her mother.

Britt nodded at my other inmates before drawing me to the far corner of the dining room, where geometric shapes were mounted on the wall.

I was almost glad she didn't reach for my hands. They'd grown sweaty in the few seconds I'd spent thinking about her mom. Also, I wanted Brittany to stay. As much as I never wanted to see another person ever again, I still didn't want Britt to leave. Go figure.

Besides, it would be understandable if Britt wanted to block my number and pretend we'd never met.

"Um." I realized I'd been staring at the floor. Had Brittany said anything? If she had, I hadn't heard her. Trying to meet her gaze, I found looking into those deep brown eyes was too much for me. I couldn't concentrate. "Will you..." I had to ask. I couldn't stop now. "...want to see me...um...ever again?"

The question hung in the air, though Brittany opened her mouth to answer immediately. Then it happened. Even more fantastic timing.

"What's this the sheriff told me about you being held hostage?"

"Mom!" Britt said, an octave higher than usual.

Even without any warning, it would have been obvious she was Brittany's mother. While there were streaks of white in her hair and some wrinkles, her brown eyes and shiny black hair were the same. Britt was taller and didn't have Mrs. Asato's almost haunted look, but the genetics were clear.

I ran a hand through my hair. Like good hair was what Mrs. Asato cared about.

My sister's mouth hung open as Britt's mom marched into the dining room—at least Juniper wasn't filming.

"Why didn't you call?" Mrs. Asato's voice wavered between hurt and anger.

Brittany jutted her chin out. "I was working."

Mrs. Asato wasn't impressed. "You're on vacation."

"I still checked on Holt's jaw." At that, Mrs. Asato leveled me with her undivided and *unimpressed* attention. So much for fixing my hair.

Brittany tried to explain with additional information. "Or, I had to give my statement to the sheriff. I'm fine. There was no need to call."

Britt's mom wasn't distracted. "He's a grown man. He should be able to take care of himself."

While it was lovely being trapped in a corner while my date argued with her mother over my competency, I reminded myself I was a semi-responsible adult and spoke up. Brittany wouldn't have spent the afternoon facedown on the floor if I hadn't invited her. Mrs.

Asato should know I took responsibility for my contribution to the afternoon.

"I'm so sorry this happened to Brittany." I willed my face to show all the regret and shame I felt about the incident. For a moment her eyes softened, and since she didn't interrupt, I continued. "We haven't been formally introduced. I'm Holt Jacobs."

"I know who you are," she spat.

While it's understandably hard to charm any parent given the circumstances, this was going worse than I imagined.

"Okay," Brittany said. "We should be going."

A mother-daughter stare-off followed, Brittany trying to get her mom to give us some privacy while Mrs. Asato made it clear the only way she was leaving was with Brittany in front of her.

Was this the last time I'd ever see Britt? I wasn't getting an answer to my question.

Pressing her lips together, Brittany conceded defeat. Then, smiling politely, she said, "Thank you for...lunch."

I nodded. Even if I'd known where Britt and I stood (which I didn't), wording an appropriate answer would have remained impossible with Britt's mom glowering at me.

Brittany nodded at Darren and Juniper on her way out—Jude had left during the family drama. Britt's eyes met mine for one final moment before she left with her mom close on her heels.

Britt's dreadlock friend ran up to me. "Hang in there. Paul and I are rooting for you." She was so short, I had to bend down when she wobbled on tippy-toes to press a quick kiss on my cheek in the way only someone who wore organic deodorant could pull off. With that, she was gone.

"Was her name Sierra?"

"Sienna," Juniper and Darren said together.

I don't know why I asked. It didn't matter.

Sagging against the wall, I took a deep breath. In all the thousands of possible date disasters, having the house ransacked while we lay facedown in the dining room had never been an option. And I'd wished Seattle was closer to Amelia's Haven. Turns out, any time I was in the same place as Brittany, my life became total mayhem. Maybe that distance was the only thing keeping our almost relationship afloat.

"So," Juniper said.

"So?"

"How was your date?" she asked.

I groaned.

Juniper giggled, and I glared at her.

"Look on the bright side. Now you've met her family."

And what a joy that had been.

CHAPTER 4

I n the five minutes after Brittany left, I checked my phone every other second. It was irrational, borderline pathetic, yet I kept checking.

Could I casually message Brittany?

Nope. There were no casual messages that could be sent five minutes after your almost girlfriend gets dragged away by her mother.

What I needed was a distraction to keep me from staring at my phone.

Technically, I could shower. But I didn't.

It was unlikely the robbers would return in the ten minutes I was naked. Still, I wasn't ready to risk it. If that made me paranoid, so be it.

The thugs had been looking for something and had run off because of Jude and Juniper's arrival. Presumably, whatever they wanted was still in the building.

Investigation would be a good distraction, so I followed in the robbers' footsteps and tore the house apart.

Well, I didn't literally tear it apart. The thugs' searching methods had leaned toward the chaotic, and I chose the more cerebral method. Which is why Darren found me in his room tapping the walls.

"Hey, buddy. What's going on here?"

I straightened. In Seattle, I'm a well-paid engineer. And have earned the reputation of someone who doesn't wander from room to room tapping on walls. Using my professional voice, I said, "I'm making an independent inquiry as to the whereabouts of previously undiscovered items."

Darren shook his head, a smile stretching across his face. "So, you're on a treasure hunt?"

"Possibly."

"Okay." Darren put his hands on his hips like he was a low-budget superhero. "Where do we start?"

I'd already gone through the fourth-floor loft, which was reachable only by a ladder made out of pipes screwed into the wall. That room was so small it hadn't taken very long. The mattress was on the floor, and the ceilings were so low I could only stand up straight in a couple of spots.

So once Darren and I finished checking his room's walls and floors, we investigated the third-floor bathroom. He hadn't been kidding. There really was no toilet paper, only the bidet.

We were very methodical as we searched every room. Yet we didn't find any wall safes behind paintings or secret openings under floorboards. Whatever the intruders were hoping to find was no longer in The Hive.

Flopping on the living room couch, which was more fashionable than comfortable, I let myself check my phone. A message had popped up from Brittany. All it said was *I'll call you later.*

That was it? No hints as to what she was thinking? No time frame? Just, *I'll call later*? What's *later*? And people say I'm cold.

I typed an overly needy reply and deleted it. An overly apologetic reply was also deleted. In the end, all I sent was a classy thumbs-up, then held my phone so I could answer the moment Britt called. Not pathetic at all.

Darren put on a Jason Statham movie that I couldn't remember if I'd seen before. Juniper sat beside me, and I found an almost comfortable semi-reclined position on the couch.

I dozed through the final action sequence, and my grip on the phone loosened. The problem was the movie ended, and I remembered I was stuck in an unsafe cabin in the middle of the woods. There wasn't any pirate treasure hidden in the floorboards. But did the burglars know that, or would they return?

The only protection came from The Local Sheriff, who probably moonlighted at a bait shop. Well, there was also Jude. I'd never considered this before, but was Jude scary? The way my brother-in-law prowled around the ground floor checking windows reminded me of the guy who'd done a rolling somersault at the first sign of intruders.

Even if Jude was James Bond, it didn't matter. I felt exposed.

The Hive had massive windows with no curtains, which was fine in daylight. But the darker it grew outside, the more I felt like a goldfish trapped in a fishbowl. Someone could be lurking just outside the large windows completely camouflaged by darkness, and I'd have no way of knowing.

"Let's get your bags," Darren said.

I jumped.

Turns out I'd been concentrating too hard on the outside to notice someone standing beside me.

What had Darren said?

Bags. Right. In all the excitement, I'd forgotten to bring my luggage inside.

Nodding to the door, Darren said, "Come on."

I pretended I wasn't paranoid being in the woods after dark, and Darren pretended I actually needed help with my luggage. We played our parts exceptionally well, though we fooled no one.

Darren ended up with my suitcase, while I carried my messenger bag. We were both heading for the stairs when Juniper intercepted me. "You never told me how you and Brittany ended up taking vacations at the same time."

How did Juniper plan when to pounce? She'd waited for the perfect time, when I was more tired than cranky. It was annoying.

I shrugged. "She invited me."

"So, out of the blue, she just invites you on her vacation?"

I shifted past Juniper to get to the stairs. "Something like that."

Juniper tilted her head. "And you didn't find it suspicious?"

"No, I didn't find it suspicious." Irritation crept into my voice—not that Juniper cared. "I'm an all-round delight to be around. Why wouldn't she want me nearby?"

Juniper raised her eyebrows. "Would you relax? I didn't call you a loser. But didn't you find the timing kind of...sudden?"

"I called you out of the blue and asked if you'd join my vacation."

Juniper pointed a finger in my face. "Yes, and I found that suspicious." She shouldn't be acting like I'd just proven her point.

Frowning, I said, "So you're suggesting her sudden invitation means she somehow orchestrated a break-in while she was in the house to give herself a perfect alibi?"

"Whatever," Juniper said, rolling her eyes. "Be a butt."

I gave an annoying older-brother grin. "Oh, I plan to."

As I started up the stairs, Jude appeared behind me, following like a silent bodyguard. I shouldn't have been relieved, but I was.

On the second-floor landing, I paused at the door of the master suite. There were Juniper's, Jude's, and Chouzie's bags neatly lined up at the foot of the bed. I didn't have the energy to argue with Juniper about bedrooms.

Sighing, I went up to the third floor, where Darren's luggage was set up in the second bedroom across from the bathroom. I really was overtired because it wasn't until that moment that I realized I was expected to sleep in the loft, with a ceiling so low I couldn't stand straight.

I shook my head. After renting the house, I ended up in the attic.

My life had become a *Goldilocks* retelling. Except, instead of finding the *just right* option, I ended up in the worst spot.

Darren was climbing down the ladder, and he slapped my back. "Good night," he said.

I eyed the ladder made of pipes. I didn't want to sleep in the attic. I didn't want to have to climb down a ladder for a cup of coffee. But I was too tired to tell Juniper or Darren they'd have to switch rooms. Besides, how would anyone get a chow chow into the loft?

Jude was talking quietly, and I hadn't paid attention to the first few sentences.

"...checked the doors and took additional precautions. No one's getting in tonight."

I didn't answer.

"Holt?"

"Yeah?"

My brother-in-law leaned toward me and, for the second time in one day, looked me straight in the eye. Was Jude always this intense? Maybe I liked it better when we didn't talk. Juniper was obviously into his intense vampire deal, but it wasn't for me. "My wife's sleeping here. Trust me. Nothing bad will happen."

There was something in his stance and tone that had me nodding. "Got it. Thanks." He was almost to the stairs when I called, "What's your job again?"

"Good night" was all he said.

When I woke up the next morning, my phone greeted me with a missed call from Brittany and no voicemail. The call came in at 9:01 p.m. When had I gone to bed? So much of yesterday's events were blurry in a way even coffee wouldn't clarify.

My mom had also sent a few texts on my family's group chat.

Depending on the day, I would skim (or outright ignore) the messages. Most of the texts were nothing more than humble brags. Juniper standing by someone who was supposedly famous. Or my other sister, Casey, giving the newest big accomplishment of her two kids—like being able to write your name is something we should all be excited about.

I read Mom's messages. Not because I was avoiding Brittany but because my parents were experiencing a midlife crisis and moving to Australia. So far Casey and Juniper were better at pretending to be supportive.

The last time I ignored the group chat, Mom almost donated a cool object from my childhood—picture something less nerdy than a replica of Aragorn's sword. They weren't selling their house but renting it furnished while storing personal belongings in the basement. Still, with Mom and Dad's departure happening in a couple of weeks, who knew what other childhood relics Mom had on the chopping block.

In the end, Mom wanted to know how I was doing after Juniper sent a picture of Chouzie in the cabin—I replied with a classy thumbs-up.

With nothing else to do, I hovered my finger over the call button by Brittany's name. It wasn't even 7:00 a.m., and we were all on vacation. Better to text. I rewrote a message seven times before settling on *Hey, sorry I missed you. Went to bed early. Call whenever.*

Pressing send, I tried not to worry about how I sounded. Too bland? Was generic better than desperate?

No one else was up. Granted, they'd all gone to bed after nine.

While making the inaugural first pot of coffee, my gaze wandered to the back door. There was a massive deck overlooking Lake Coeur d'Alene just outside. It would be a stunning view for a morning cup of coffee. But I'd spend the whole time worrying about men in neon gaiters emerging from the trees. Also, who knew what extra precautions Jude had taken. I could be booby-trapped inside.

This was ridiculous. I'd spent an obscene amount of money to stay here and was too scared to go outside. Still, I had my reasons. No disrespect to The Local Sheriff, but I doubted a break-in where nothing was stolen would be her top priority.

Filling the biggest mug I could find, I sat on the couch and tried my best to get comfortable. I double-checked my phone after a few sips of coffee. Nothing new from Brittany.

Trying to focus on yesterday's break-in, I analyzed the specifics.

First off, the burglars had been hunting for something in particular. They could have had my wallet or, for that matter, my car.

Second, they had a code to get in. There was a slight chance they were the last tenants, and the code hadn't been erased. It was a remote possibility if something valuable was lost. Of course, that wouldn't explain why they'd ransacked all the bags. Especially Chouzie's. Why bother with chew toys and overpriced grooming equipment?

The whole thing reeked of an inside job.

Time to meet my suspects. Pulling up the confirmation email, I tapped on the link for Camarata Properties. Beneath the company's logo, a breezy font with the barest outline of a building, was a portrait of a family so attractive, I hoped it was photoshopped. There was a generic blurb about how Patrick Camarata had founded the business thirty-plus years ago, and it had grown and expanded with the support of his loving family. There were photos of the different employees and their job titles. Good ol' Patrick was the king of the castle, while his second wife, Megan, daughter, Gina, and an assortment of extended family were all in key management positions. After the family section, there were tons of headshots full of employee names and titles. Were my intruders among this group of people?

Halfway down the page, I paused at the name Travis Jones. Where had I seen that name?

On a hunch, I checked my confirmation email. The signature at the bottom belonged to Travis Jones. Even from the headshot, it was clear he didn't fit the runway looks of the Camarata family. He had a bushy beard and was big and scary in a rugged, meat-and-potatoes, has-skinned-a-raccoon sort of way.

Matching the name with the face had probably been a waste of time. Travis had rented me The Hive. So he definitely knew the building was occupied and wouldn't have broken in.

What I really needed was the information stored in the Camarata Properties client software. It was 7:30 a.m. Calling the rental office before 8:00 a.m. would bring me to a rarely checked voicemail. Or (even worse) an answering service with people who wasted ten minutes asking random questions before deciding they couldn't help.

I'd run out of investigating, and Brittany was still radio silent. So I did what any responsible man would do: took a shower and styled my hair.

But after the shower I had to climb back up the ridiculous pipe ladder before I could choose a suitably sexy-casual summer look. I settled on a designer pair of plaid shorts and a monogrammed white polo from a golf course Dad had taken me to.

In the time I'd spent upstairs, Juniper and Chouzie had gotten up and taken over the living room. Juniper was creating content for both her and Chouzie's followers—the price of fame.

Juniper was busy announcing the dognappers hadn't returned and Chouzie was still safe when I saw I'd missed another call from Brittany during my shower. How hard was it to get dumped?

My finger hovered over the redial. But for some reason I couldn't call. I didn't want it to be over. So I took the coward's way out and sent a text saying I was out of the shower.

The front door was now open, with nothing but a screen made to stop mosquitoes protecting us from the villains at Camarata Properties.

At least the door wasn't booby-trapped.

Not wanting to start trending as Juniper's *#grumpybrother*, I refilled my coffee cup, got my sunglasses, and went out to the front porch. The front deck only had a view of the road and pine trees, but it was the safer option. I couldn't relax looking at the boats in the lake if the whole time I was checking the bushes for thugs in neon gaiters.

It was a little after 8:00 a.m. when I stepped outside, and I planned to call Travis at Camarata Properties. But before I could call, I heard footsteps. At first they were so faint I thought I was hearing things. Then came a creak and someone was walking up the porch steps.

Whirling around to face my intruder, I ended up spilling half my coffee on the pristine deck. There was a half second of panic, during which I considered vaulting off the deck and crash-landing on the ground; then I recognized Britt.

So I didn't need to make a second attempt at being James Bond. Lucky me.

Instinctively, I grinned. Then, remembering she might be calling off our friendship, I frowned. But then I really looked like Juniper's #grumpybrother, so I forced my face to look somewhat neutral and even took off my sunglasses.

"Morning," I said.

A nervous smile played on Brittany's mouth. "Morning," she said.

"Um"—I ran a hand through my previously perfect hair—"can I get you coffee or tea?"

"No. Thanks."

I gestured toward an overly geometric bench that belonged in the lobby of a modern art museum, and we both sat.

And sat.

Until it really got uncomfortable.

I started to say, "I'm really sorry about—"

Right as Britt said, "My mom isn't usually—"

We both stopped to let the other person talk. Then, with a new silence threatening, I decided to let Britt off easy. "I really like you," I said and couldn't stop the grin. "I still really like you. But after yesterday, I understand if you'd want us to go our separate ways."

"What?" Brittany's eyes darted around as she processed what I said. Then her eyes sparkled. "So you really like me?"

"Um...yeah." Was I blushing?

Britt's eyes hardened for a second, outlining the scar by her eyebrow. It was quickly replaced by sadness. The next second she was smiling. "I really like you too." She slid closer to me on the bench. "After my mom charged in, I didn't know if you'd want to see me again."

I rolled my eyes. "Remember when we met, I had you give my mom a doctor's note?"

Britt laughed. "That's fair." Her eyes grew distant. "This time of year is tough for Mom. She really took everything surrounding Jeremy's death hard. Seeing the sheriff after I'd been gone for so long brought that to the surface."

I nodded, unsure of the right words for such a confession.

"So," I said, deciding it best to change the subject. "Now that we've established we both still like each other, was there another reason for your visit?"

"Oh." Brittany flushed like she'd been caught in a lie. "I thought you were avoiding my calls, so I came for a face-to-face conversation."

I didn't hide my frown. "I wasn't avoiding anything."

"You were actually asleep before 9:00 p.m.?"

How should I explain?

"Uh...I'd had a long drive and a lot had happened...There were so many people..." My face gave the best proof of my early bedtime.

Britt's eyes twinkled. "Sorry, Grandpa. My mistake."

Grandpa wasn't my favorite nickname, but I'd let it go this time.

I took a long drink of coffee. "Since yesterday's lunch was a no-go, how about I make breakfast?"

"I don't know. You did burn the onions," she said, her tone flirting, "and Jude's cooking was pretty good."

"Hey! All he did was cook the food I'd already prepared."

"Wait." Britt's frown returned. "After yesterday's break-in, weren't you planning on going to the rental office?"

I didn't answer Britt. She'd already been in accidental peril. I didn't want her tagging along while I asked people, *Hey, did you break into my house yesterday?*

Britt's eyes narrowed. "You already have a plan."

I tried to hide my face with the mug. But it was too late. Britt was onto me.

CHAPTER 5

I was definitely in trouble, but not about the break-in.

My investigation was well under way. I'd called, and an overly perky front desk worker informed me that Travis the Big and Scary would be in the office after nine. She didn't call him *big* or *scary*, but based off the width of his shoulders, he was both.

The real problem was the trip had just started, and already it was difficult to imagine leaving Brittany. Seattle is so far away from Amelia's Haven. How would virtual dating work? Friday nights spent sipping wine over webcams?

While I was busy brooding about the future, Brittany suggested we walk to the Camarata Properties office in Baycliff.

Mrs. Asato's horrified face flashed through my mind. It would be nice if she liked me. So I shrugged and said, "Walking will slow us down. I don't know when you have to be back with your family."

Britt's paramedic mask covered her face for a moment before being replaced by an expression a little too carefree. "No rush," she said.

Yikes. Juniper was right. Brittany was hiding something. But it wasn't my business. Britt could tell me if she wanted to. Putting on my sunglasses, I said, "Okay," and we headed to town.

The walk to Baycliff was pleasant enough. Walking through town highlighted all the red, white, and blue for the upcoming holiday.

We were a couple of blocks away from Camarata Properties when Brittany left the sidewalk for an abandoned parking lot. Well, abandoned except for a ratty shack on wheels. I was wondering why she'd be going toward an abandoned trailer when I read the sign.

FIREWORKS.

Brittany liked fireworks?

"Britt?" I asked, not believing my eyes.

She couldn't be into fireworks. They were recklessly dangerous.

"Britt?" I asked again.

"Don't look at me like that." Her lips quirked. "They're fireworks, not grenades."

She did like fireworks? I took a step back. "Hold on. How many calls have you gotten where someone lost a finger because they got too excited playing with firecrackers?"

At first Brittany didn't answer, and when she did, her words were overly precise. "I've never worked a dismemberment."

The way she'd answered was like a witness coached on the stand, and I was onto her. "So no missing fingers, but you do get more calls around fireworks season?"

"Well..." Brittany swayed a little from side to side. "I'm very safe when I light off fireworks."

I forced my smirk into a frown. "Avoiding the question? I've got a hostile witness."

Brittany shook her head, but her eyes sparkled. "Trust me, they're fun."

"Call me vain. But I like having all my fingers."

Brittany squeezed her eyes shut. "You're impossible," she said, more to herself than to me. Then she added, "Lucky for you, this stand isn't open for a few more hours."

Britt returned to the sidewalk, and I jogged to catch up. "But you plan on coming back?"

"Obviously."

Twenty-four hours in the same location as Britt, and I discovered she was a pyro. What would another day reveal?

"Holt, don't make that face."

I arched an eyebrow.

"Come on," she said. "Do you know how many days a year you can legally light off fireworks?"

"Seattle? Never. Other places? Depends on local laws."

Brittany shook her head. "July third and fourth from nine a.m. to eleven p.m. Two days out of the year to shoot fire up into the sky. You have to admit it's magical."

I shook my head. "It's dangerous. I mean"—I ran a hand through my hair—"I avoid sparklers if I can help it."

Brittany had no response.

Was this our first fight?

"They sometimes look cool," I said, trying to be less of a jerk.

"Well"—Brittany tucked invisible strands of hair behind her ears—"last year Sienna and I did fireworks over the lake on the third, and then we all drove up to Coeur d'Alene for the city's firework show on the Fourth. I thought you might like to be a part of it, but if it makes you too nervous..."

"Brittany"—my voice had an unexpected growl to it—"if you'll be there, I'll be there."

I froze.

I sounded like a serial killer.

Thankfully, Britt didn't seem bothered. She blushed slightly and kept walking.

"Wait," I said, catching up. "Will your mom be upset with me joining the group for Coeur d'Alene's fireworks?"

"I mean..." Brittany shrugged. "She should get used to you."

Instead of being freaked out, I grinned. "All right. It's a date."

When we entered the office of Camarata Properties, I made a horrifying discovery. Everyone in the office was wearing plaid flannel button-ups. Plaid flannel...*in July?* Was plaid flannel the company dress code, or had it happened accidentally? Which is worse?

Nothing else was particularly noteworthy in the space. The furniture was from the nineties, and they were going for folksy charm. How had such an organization ever built The Hive?

Since I'd called ahead, they were more or less expecting us, and it didn't take long for Travis to appear from the back hallway. His employee headshot hadn't done him justice. He was huge and moved with the confidence of someone who spends a lot of time outdoors.

Travis gave us a once-over before extending a large hand. "I'm Travis Jones."

We started to shake as I said, "Holt Jacobs."

His grip tightened for a second; then his mouth did what I assume was a smile but was swallowed in his beard. "From Seattle?"

"Uh..." I'd never mentioned Seattle in our emails. "How did you know?"

Travis's beard hid his expression, and his tone didn't give anything away. "Just a guess." He moved on to Brittany but didn't creepily guess where she was from.

What about me showed I was from Seattle? The sunglasses? A sense of style? It's not like my polo was monogrammed with the Space Needle.

It was a short walk to his office. The room was small, and the only personal touch was a pair of muddy hiking shoes in the corner. Brittany sat across from Travis while I stood beside her.

"What seems to be the problem?" he asked.

Brittany and I detailed yesterday's ordeal. If Travis was surprised, he hid it behind his beard. Had The Local Sheriff even bothered to notify Camarata Properties?

Once we were done, Travis said, "My sincerest apologies." The words were spoken with as much sincerity as if they were memorized from the employee handbook.

Did the handbook have a break-ins section?

Britt didn't seem bothered and asked, "Could you check what code was used to enter the back door yesterday afternoon?"

Travis hesitated, and emotion almost showed through the beard. "Look, aren't the police handling this?"

Britt leaned forward. "How are we supposed to enjoy our vacation with this hanging over us?"

Travis closed his eyes and took a deep breath before saying, "It's not policy to—"

"Don't give me that." Heat rose in Britt's cheeks. "Did you know a social media icon is staying at The Hive? One word from her could cause quite a scandal."

Whoa. Britt fought dirty.

Annoyance flashed across Travis's eyes, then something that resembled admiration. He nodded. "Of course." A few keystrokes later, he said, "The code used was this month's master code. All employees get the code so they can access rooms for cleaning and maintenance needs."

So it was an inside job. I'd been right.

Then I replayed what Travis had said. Everyone in the company used the same code? How was that a good idea? They were opening themselves up to so many security risks.

I opened my mouth to make a few suggestions, but Brittany took my hand and gave it a quick squeeze.

"Interesting," I said, managing to keep my full-blown rant on the inside.

Giving Travis a more thorough inspection, I was positive he was too big to be one of the people who'd broken in. Definitely not Mr. Bear, who'd been guarding us. His forearm was covered by the flannel shirt, but if Travis had punched me, my jaw would have been shattered instead of bruised.

"Do any of your coworkers have a bear tattoo on their forearm?" I asked.

Surprise flashed across Travis's face, but it was gone the next instant. He shrugged. "A lot of people here have tattoos. Some bears and trees. Even a few fish tattoos."

Fish? Who wanted fish permanently inked on their body?

I was getting distracted. Time to ask the question that could have kept me up all night if I didn't suffer from reverse insomnia. "Who was supposed to rent The Hive? How did you get them to let me rent it instead?"

Travis's jaw ticked. "That's confidential."

I should have thought of that. "Right." I considered using Britt's blackmail threat but didn't have the stomach for it. "Well, do you have any idea what the renters were bringing?"

Travis glanced toward the door, a not-so-subtle invitation for us to leave. "Why would their luggage matter?" he asked.

Was this guy for real?

"Since nothing was taken, I assumed the thieves were expecting to find something specific."

When Travis didn't immediately reply, Brittany added, "Nothing was stolen, but the whole house was torn apart."

Travis's eyes lingered on Brittany, considering what she said. Something about the way he suddenly looked away made it clear he was hiding something. All he said was, "I'm not a mind reader."

I really should look up interrogation tactics. There had to be a way to get Travis to tell us what he knew.

Unexpectedly, the office door was flung open, and Mr. Camarata stood there in plaid flannel. He had the look of a handsome man in a soap commercial. Or he would have if his face weren't red with fury. "Where are my diamonds?"

Wow. My jaw didn't exactly drop at his entrance, but I definitely wasn't expecting that.

"Sir." Travis was immediately on his feet. "I'm meeting with Holt and Brittany about the break-in they had at The Hive."

"Yeah, yeah." He waved off Travis's words. "They shouldn't be there. It was reserved. Where are the diamonds?"

There was movement behind Mr. C. in the hallway. "Daddy, it's okay. It's not Travis's fault," a woman was saying.

"Um." Travis's eyes traveled from Mr. C. to the woman in the hallway, to me, to the floor, to the ceiling, then back to Mr. Camarata. "There was a booking error." Mr. C. opened his mouth, but Travis kept talking. "It's only this week. I caught the error and moved the valuables to the pool house."

A new voice came from the hallway. "Mr. Camarata, if you could return to your office, we'll finish the interview." From the tone, I guessed it was The Local Sheriff. So she was investigating. Shocking.

Mr. C. walked farther into the office and hit Travis with the icy glare of a CEO. "So you're telling me, Travis, when I look at the accounts, there will be payments from these two?"

"Daddy, please." A stunning woman with big brown eyes entered and began tugging at Mr. C.'s arm like she was a little kid. "Be nice. We're getting married in ten days."

Mr. Camarata ignored his daughter, his eyes trained on Travis.

"Yes, sir," Travis said, standing his ground. "Like I said, it was a booking error."

I tried to take a deep breath. There really wasn't space in the office for me, Britt, Travis, Mr. C., and Mr. C.'s daughter. The Local Sheriff moving to stand at the entrance made the room that much smaller.

She said, "Now that you got that cleared up, I have a few more questions."

"Mr. Camarata"—a new head crowded into the doorframe—"was I still driving you to the meeting?" The man's face came into focus, and a second later, his pupils were dilating. But from what or who in the suffocatingly small room?

"Yes, Scott. Thank you." The redness was fading from Mr. Camarata's face, and the monster of a minute ago was now a respectable businessman. "If you'll excuse me," he said, nodding to everyone in the room as he left.

His big-eyed daughter rushed to embrace Travis the Big and Scary. "I'm so sorry, babe. You know how Daddy can get."

Travis visibly relaxed as he held his fiancée. He talked over her head to Britt and me, his free hand gesturing to the door. "I trust I've answered all your questions. Gina and I have wedding details to work out."

Actually, he hadn't answered my questions. But the man had just played the bride card. If I were alone, I might have ignored the *don't stress the bride* rule. But with Brittany, I muttered, "Thanks," and we left Travis's office.

We ran into The Local Sheriff, who'd been abandoned in the hallway. "I didn't expect to see you here," she said.

Were we in trouble?

"Uh, yeah," I said, putting on my sunglasses and opening the exit door for Britt and the sheriff. "I wanted to know how someone used a code to break in."

The Local Sheriff gave an unprofessional snort. "If you solve that, you'll be able to close a few more thefts on Camarata Properties. They have one master code. It kind of opens them up to burglaries."

"Burglaries?"

The sheriff pressed her lips together. "Never mind." Then she added, "Yours was different anyway. You were in the house, and nothing was taken." Abruptly she turned to her patrol car.

"Bye," Brittany called, and the sheriff gave a half wave.

I let out a deep breath.

Brittany half smiled. "You good?"

"No," I said. "I need coffee."

Since the town was too small to have a recognizable coffee chain, my options were Baycliff's Brew or waiting until I'd hiked back to the rental. So I shopped local.

And...well...there's a reason I usually don't shop local.

I get that I'm not an example of Baycliff's average townie or tourist. Still, it's a wonder Baycliff's Brew was in business.

First no one was at the counter. Then, when a guy did wander over, he looked at me funny when I ordered a latte.

When it was Brittany's turn, she ordered black tea. Was Britt a tea drinker? Now I was giving her a funny look. Tea drinking was an issue I'd need to discuss at a later date.

There was no way I was staying at Baycliff's Brew one minute longer than it took to get my drink. I practically ditched Brittany in my hurry to get out of there.

Taking a seat on a public bench, I stretched out my legs and took a couple of gulps of coffee.

Britt sat beside me. "How's that?"

I shrugged, beginning to relax. "The coffee could be stronger."

Brittany tossed her hair back. "You say that about all the blends."

I raised an eyebrow and took another drink.

I'd been so distracted by a company using one master code for all its employees that I hadn't considered everything else I'd learned.

Mr. C. had asked about diamonds, not people.

Had The Hive somehow been reserved for the sole purpose of storing diamonds? That sounded ridiculous. Yet nothing about Baycliff or Camarata Properties was normal.

Were those diamonds the reason I ate a faceful of floor yesterday? If the sheriff was to be believed, the Camaratas had a history of master codes being used to rob their rentals.

Beside me, Britt made a strange sound in the back of her throat. She was frowning down at her phone. Tons of notifications covered the screen, and there was an incoming call from *Mom* that she ignored. Britt shoved the phone into her pocket. "We should go."

"Don't you want to get that?" I tried to sound teasing. This had happened a few weeks ago, only I'd been the one ducking family calls.

Brittany sighed. "We'll be back soon enough."

Strange. Ignoring family calls was my style. I didn't think it was Britt's.

What was going on?

Leaving the bench, we started the walk back. I wanted to talk about Mr. Camarata's diamonds, Travis's fiancée, and The Local Sheriff's comments about similar crimes. But Brittany's face had an unusual tension, so we walked in silence.

Even then, I had plenty to do trying to go at the same speed as Britt. One minute she was speed-walking, and the next she was moving slower than my grandma window-shopping.

"What's going on?" I finally asked when it had gotten too ridiculous.

"Hm? Oh. Sorry." Brittany had been racing down the road and slowed to what she probably thought was a normal speed. A couple of yards later, she changed speeds again, and I reminded myself to be patient.

We were nearly to The Hive when Brittany stopped walking altogether. "Why was Travis so weird?"

Even though my thoughts had wandered down a similar path, I'd assumed she was thinking about her mom. I shrugged. "He's probably protecting someone or hiding something. Maybe a friend or his fiancée's family. He is marrying into the Camarata empire."

"We should follow him." Britt said those words as casually as she might have said, *it's a sunny day*, then continued walking like the matter was settled.

"Hold on." I jogged to catch up. "Are you suggesting we stalk a man who's probably killed countless animals with his bare hands?"

Britt's face had a stubborn set I didn't recognize. "*Tailing*, not *stalking*," she said.

"Remind me of the difference?"

Britt ignored my question. "He clearly knew the guy with the bear tattoo. Travis might try to talk to him. Then we'd have our main suspect."

I ran a hand through my hair, unsure what to say.

"I can tail him by myself," Britt said when I'd been silent for too long.

"So you're suggesting we sit in a car all day in case Travis sneaks out the back door to have a whispered conversation with one of our intruders?"

"Holt—" Britt cut off what she was going to say and, after a glance to the sky, said, "I'm busy all afternoon. But I'm going by the Camaratas' office at closing to see if I catch him leaving."

This wasn't making any sense. Between the two of us, Britt's the reasonable, levelheaded one. "Uh," I said as we reached The Hive.

Instead of stopping, I kept walking, deciding to drop her off at her place and buy myself a few more minutes to think. Did she just want an excuse to be alone with me? If that were the case, I was all in. But the set of her jaw and the scar by her eyebrow indicated she didn't have romance on her mind.

At Britt's cabin, I ran out of time. A group of women were gathered on the front porch. Sienna looked happy to see us, while Mrs. Asato's face paled. How much more would Britt's mom dislike me if she found out I'd let Brittany stalk Travis the Big and Scary by herself? What if something happened? I cleared my throat, the right decision becoming obvious. "Your car or mine?"

"I'd better pick you up," Britt said, blushing. "Mom would freak out if she saw me getting into a car with *the home invader.*"

I groaned. "I didn't invade my own home!"

Britt's mouth quirked. "Try telling her."

CHAPTER 6

Chouzie was the only one to greet me when I got back to The Hive. He walked up to me with his blue-black tongue hanging out and did a lap around my legs before returning to his dog bed by the couch.

I let out a breath, glad for the quiet. What was up with Brittany? We'd been video-calling a lot the past few weeks, and this stubborn, secretive side was different.

Come to think of it, Juniper was right. Britt's invitation had been forced. I'd been too excited to notice. What exactly was going on?

There was a rustling sound deeper in the house. My stomach clenched. Was anyone else here? Had there been vehicles parked out front? If the intruders had returned, this time I'd be armed with something more than a spatula. Unfortunately, there were limited options. Detaching a mirrored sphere from the wall, I checked the dining room, bathroom, and kitchen before heading upstairs. The master bedroom and bathroom were clear. Then, as I reached the third-floor landing, a figure emerged from one of the rooms.

Yelling, I chucked the mirrored sphere at the intruder. A moment later, I recognized Darren.

He easily caught the sphere, then grinned at me. "Maybe spend less time at the gym and more time learning martial arts."

"Whatever." The danger was over, but my heart was pounding in my ears, and I had to steady myself against the wall. "Why are you here?" I grumbled.

Thankfully, Darren ignored the obvious answer—that he was at The Hive because I'd invited him. "I'm getting better shoes," he said, kneeling to finish tying one of the laces. "Juniper is having us investigate the back porch and dock for clues."

Juniper? Had the investigating bug bit everyone this trip?

I followed Darren outside to the back deck, since having either Darren or Juniper suspect I was scared to go behind the house would be very damaging and could lead to future blackmailing.

"Holt!" Juniper jogged up, almost quivering with energy. "We're searching for any clues your dastardly villains may have left."

"I heard." My voice was neutral, and the sunglasses hid the panic in my eyes. What was I expecting? Monsters to jump out of the trees like jack-in-the-boxes? "What have you found, Dr. Watson?"

Juniper crinkled her nose. "You're Sherlock in this relationship?"

"Yeah. Between the two of us, who has solved more crimes?"

"Mm." Juniper tilted her head. "What I remember is helping you piece together clues that left you stumped and warning you not to self-sabotage your love life."

Huh.

Juniper's order of events wasn't exactly accurate. But there was enough truth in what she said that I didn't have a comeback.

Taking my arm, Juniper ushered me off the porch. "*My dear Watson,*" she said like she'd won the case. "As you can see, to the left and right go dirt paths that lead between the different cabins. It would have been easy enough to sneak up unseen." Her tone was professional, like she was a detective from one of the cop shows she used to watch with

Mom. "I have my two best men patrolling both directions for possible clues."

Had she become BFFs with Darren? And if Darren and Jude were her best men, what did that make me?

"After a brief examination"—Juniper continued her cop talk—"there are obvious signs of disuse on both sides of the trail. My theory is they came by sea."

Technically not the sea. It was a lake. But I'd let it slide for the sake of her character.

"Keep your eyes open, Sergeant," Juniper tried to bark as we made our way down a steep footpath with a couple of switchbacks leading to the water.

Was random police sergeant a demotion from Dr. Watson?

Demotions aside, it didn't take long for me to get into the spirit of things. Juniper's commitment was contagious, and I was studying the path and surrounding foliage as intently as she was.

At the final switchback there was a gap in the pebbles and a few indents. "Here," I called. "Someone tripped."

Juniper and I examined the spot.

"I didn't see anyone when I came around the house yesterday. I must have just missed them," Juniper said.

"It would be easy to stumble if you came down this hill in a hurry." I imitated trying to make the switchback's turn at a run and found snapped twigs that someone had grabbed to slow the fall. "Their legs could have gotten scratched."

"Were your villains wearing shorts?" Juniper asked.

How would I know?

I shrugged, "Ask Britt."

Juniper's eyes widened. "So you're still together?"

While I'd been worried about that very same point this morning, the question annoyed me. "Of course we are." I gave my best frat-boy grin. "I'm perfect."

Juniper rolled her eyes. "Right."

We made it down to the rocky shoreline and inspected our private dock but didn't find anything else out of place. I was about to suggest we head in and make some lunch, but Juniper had other plans.

"Now that we have their route mapped out, it's time to bring out Chouzie and let the world know the dognapper's escape plan."

"Juniper," I growled, her interest in detecting suddenly making sense.

"What?" She made her innocent-baby-sister face.

Whatever. I'd go along with her narrative. "If this was all about Chouzie, why didn't you bring him along? Get him to track the scent or something."

Juniper stood a little taller. "I brought him out here. But while Chouzie's ancestors may have been trackers, he hasn't been trained for it. And...well"—she wouldn't look at me—"he got away and jumped in the water. Totally wrecked his hair."

"I'll bet," I said, not quite able to sound serious.

Juniper shook her head. "This is better. I'll bring Chouzie to the water, hold on tight to his leash, and give everyone the details about the *dognapping-at-sea*...or does *dog-boat-napping* sound better?"

This time I couldn't help myself. "It's a lake, not a sea."

Juniper punched my shoulder. Real mature.

After her little act of violence, Juniper ditched me to get updates from Darren and Jude. I didn't hear much of what they said, but it didn't take a genius to know they hadn't made any discoveries.

Jude hung back to walk with me. "You find the spot where someone tripped?" he asked.

"Yep," I said. When had Jude found it? "Anything else I should know?"

Jude shook his head. "Not at this time."

The Local Sheriff hadn't even gone out back. Meanwhile, my sister and her husband weren't leaving any stone unturned. Granted, Jude's reason was safety and Juniper's was fame, but they both put the work in.

Jude caught up to Juniper on the porch and put an arm around her waist. He whispered in her ear, and she giggled.

Wait. Jude wouldn't plant evidence for Juniper to find, to help her social media...right? It sounded crazy. Still, two days ago, I'd never imagined Jude capable of somersaulting behind couches.

I spent way too much of my afternoon worrying about what to wear for my night *tailing* Travis with Brittany. Was black appropriate? Like I was a spy on a secret mission? Or should I dress up in case we ended up on a real date?

In the end, I decided to stick with my white polo and plaid shorts. I also packed a bag of snacks in case stalking went past dinnertime. Ideally, Travis would have already left work. Then I could take Brittany out for a proper meal—or as proper a meal as Baycliff could offer.

Britt picked me up at 4:45 p.m. There wasn't space in her car for my legs and the bag of snacks. I was tossing the bag onto the back seat and hadn't buckled when Brittany accelerated away from The Hive.

Getting flung into the glove box wasn't a great start. Sitting back, I buckled myself in before hitting Brittany with one of my patented glares. She was too busy checking the rearview mirror to notice.

"Are we being tailed?" I asked.

"Not exactly," Britt said, her whole body rigid.

"Awesome," I said, rubbing my elbow.

"Sorry." Britt's shoulders slumped. "It's my mom."

"I see." How much did Mrs. Asato dislike me? I couldn't be that bad. I have a good job and shower regularly.

Glancing away from the road, Britt pursed her lips. "Not you. Or not only you." A glimmer of humor flickered in her eyes. "Mom and I, plus a bunch of other ladies, including Paul's girlfriend, Sienna, made this trip a year ago. It was really good last year, but now"—she shook her head, hands gripping the steering wheel too tightly—"now I'm having Sienna create distractions while I sneak out the back."

"Wow," I said. "You're a terrible person."

"Holt!" That surprised her out of her moodiness.

Settling back in my seat, I really committed. "I'm not comfortable being in the same car with you. Please pull over. I'll walk back."

Britt's scar appeared, then disappeared as she worked through what I'd said. "The only reason we started hanging out was so you could avoid going surfing with your family."

There was the woman I'd been texting with every day. "Hm." I pretended to think it over. "I guess I'm as bad as you." I winked.

Britt tilted her head. "Trust me, you're much worse."

"Oh, I know."

Britt wasn't smiling, but she'd stopped white-knuckling the steering wheel. I took the win.

Brittany parked in the Camarata Properties lot, and we watched the door.

It was really boring.

I sat politely on my side of the car with very little legroom. Meanwhile, Brittany kept fiddling with her hair and her aqua scrunchie. Her hair was in a ponytail, then down around her shoulders, with the hair band on her wrist. She put it in a bun before taking her hair down and playing with the scrunchie.

A Tesla parked, and Mr. Camarata got out of the passenger seat. Instead of going back to the office, Mr. C. drove off in an iconic red truck—the kind transporting Christmas trees on wrapping paper.

The Tesla's driver waited until Mr. C.'s red truck had left the lot before getting out. It was the guy from the office hallway. His flannel shirt covered his forearms, so there was no way of knowing if he had a bear tattoo. After stretching, the guy went to a faded brown pickup and drove away.

They left the Tesla abandoned in the parking lot...Why drive electric when you can drive a pickup?

A couple of minutes before five, people began shuffling from the building, getting into cars, and driving away. At 5:12 p.m., the lot had emptied except for the abandoned Tesla and a green late-nineties truck.

"This was a bust," I said, popping my neck. "Do you want to get some supper?" Not the most romantic invitation, but it got the point across.

"Let's wait a little longer," she said.

I tried (unsuccessfully) not to groan. My legs were crammed against the glove box. No one else was leaving Camarata Properties, and Brittany wasn't making any move to go. I began playing with buttons and handles until I could better stretch out, before fixing the backrest and raising the headrest. When everything was just so, I sat back.

Brittany had been watching. "You're like a five-year-old."

I tried to look offended, but I didn't really care. Brittany was the one who'd suggested a stalking mission, and she was the one fiddling with an aqua scrunchie. If a poll was taken on who was behaving more maturely, this time I'd win.

Britt's phone vibrated, and she frowned when she checked it.

"Your mom?"

A smile played on her face. "Actually, Paul."

I'd only met her twin once, at a real low point in his life. "I'm surprised you all left him alone for a few days," I said.

Brittany snorted. "Oh, he was begging for it. He's been a little smothered the past couple of months." She shook her head, "Trust me, he's pulled a disappearing act way more times than me. Tomorrow he's going backpacking in the actual wilderness with a buddy while I'm trapped in an overpriced house with women who ensure my wineglass is never empty."

I shook my head, "Some guys get all the luck."

"Well—" Britt's focus was suddenly out the window. I didn't need to check to know that what I'd been dreading had occurred.

Travis the Big and Scary had appeared.

Each step he took toward his truck seemed to echo in my head. It was like a movie's slow-motion scene of impending doom. I had a bad feeling about this.

I glanced at Britt. Was she really going to tail my scary rental agent? She turned the car on. The answer was yes.

She waited a few seconds after Travis's truck had turned before she began to follow. She stayed an appropriate distance behind him, and cars in between camouflaged us.

Following a pickup through a backwoods town is more complicated than you might think, since every local is sporting their preferred brand of pickup. We almost lost him once, but unfortunately, Brittany spotted him turning onto the highway.

We began climbing up a windy mountain road, frequently losing sight of Travis's green truck with all the bends and crowding pine trees.

My stomach gave a low rumble, but instead of getting supper at an adequate restaurant, I was a passenger on a dangerous mission.

We were thirty minutes out of town when I decided to ask, "How much farther do you plan on going?"

Britt was chewing her top lip and would've played with her scrunchie if she hadn't been driving. "I don't know."

"I hope you have a full tank." I should've stayed silent. My voice was harsher than intended.

Color rose in Brittany's cheeks. "Sorry," she said. "I shouldn't have dragged you along. It's hard to explain, but I can't go back...not tonight."

Well, that was cryptic.

"Okay." I fixed my hair, thinking through what she said. "Let's drive, then. We can go anywhere. Mount Rushmore, New York, anywhere you want. But," I said, "let's leave poor Travis alone."

Britt frowned. "I know Travis lied."

"I agree, but isn't this"—I gestured out the car—"a little extra?"

Britt puffed herself up for a moment like she was ready to argue, then slumped behind the steering wheel. "Maybe," she finally said.

Luck was not on my side. Just when Britt was ready to quit stalking, the green truck slowed down, and Travis's turn signal began flashing. Like a dream, a wrought-iron gate appeared between the trees with the cursive initials *P.C.* embossed over the entrance. Once Travis drove through, the gate slid shut. A tall rock wall went along either side of the entrance, blending into the shadows and the trees.

The estate had to belong to Mr. Camarata...not that I remembered his first name. But who else would bother disturbing the forest for an ostentatious stone wall?

Britt drove past the gate, and for a moment I hoped we would have a kind of normal evening. Then she pulled off the road and parked so that we had a clear view of the gate but were somewhat hidden against the stone wall.

"Shall we take a peek inside?" Britt asked with a smile I didn't like.

What was with her?

Her hand was moving to the door.

"No," I said. "Absolutely not. Stalking is one thing, but I draw the line at trespassing."

The stubborn look was back on her face. "Come on, Holt."

I twisted my hair in my fingers. How did I talk to this person? She wasn't someone I'd dealt with before. What could I say? Then it hit me. We had a mutual enemy who didn't care about privacy. So I took my best shot. "You're acting like Dakota."

Brittany's hand jerked from the door handle like it was electrified.

I cleared my throat. "Britt?"

She wouldn't look at me.

Awkward.

Note to self, don't start disagreements in cars parked in the wilderness.

When she finally opened her mouth, it was to burst into tears.

Was she broken?

What had I done?

"Um, sorry?" I said.

Should I try to comfort her? My options were limited, with us seated in a car. Still, I reached a hand over and began doing some weird combination of stroking and patting her arm.

When her crying morphed into hysterical laughter, I moved my hand back to my side of the car. "You're right," she choked out. "Taking an unauthorized look is exactly what Dakota would do."

I wasn't exactly sure why that was funny, but I would take laughter over tears. "Plus," I added, "we're in the wilderness. I think trespassers are shot on sight out here."

Brittany began wiping at her eyes. I think she was about to apologize when my stomach growled. She smiled. "Sounds like suppertime."

"I'm prepared."

Grabbing the bag, we divvied up the food. It wasn't anything special. Baycliff's only grocery store had limited options. Besides chips and drinks, I ended up buying sandwiches from the deli section. They weren't exactly appetizing, but definitely less questionable than the sushi.

They did the trick.

Brittany drank water while I opened an energy drink. I don't usually drink them, but they seemed appropriate stakeout fuel. The meal started in silence, but over time she relaxed, and we started talking like normal. Still, she never elaborated on why she couldn't go back to her mom's cabin. I wanted to ask, but I didn't. She would tell me if she wanted to.

While I'd prefer not to sit in a parked car in the forest, I could get used to the rest of it. Chill evenings spent with Britt were becoming my favorite thing. We still had days left on our vacation, yet returning to Seattle by myself left a hollow feeling in my chest. What was there in Seattle besides a good job and a fancy apartment? Sure it was nice in theory, but the reality was pretty empty.

Where did that leave me? Moving to Amelia's Haven? I hated that place. It was an ultra-bleached tourist trap that tried way too hard to be cheery.

"Hold on," Brittany said, pulling me from my thoughts.

A light brown truck was at the gate. This time, instead of the gate immediately opening, the driver unrolled the window and began talking into the intercom. It could have been the guy who drove Mr. C. in the Tesla, but it was too far away to know for sure.

"Do you see that?"

I frowned. "I see the truck at the entrance."

"Holt, I mean the bear tattoo."

Squinting, I tried to make it out, but all I saw was a dark blur on his forearm. It could have been a bruise or even a fish tattoo.

"Are you sure?" I asked.

"Of course I'm sure."

The gate opened, and the brown truck disappeared.

"He's probably meeting with Travis," Britt said. "When he leaves, we can tail him to his partners."

"More stalking?" I groaned.

"More tailing."

I knew my fate. There was no point in trying to fight it.

We began discussing the case. The truck was probably the same light brown one we'd seen earlier. But it easily could have been a different brand of truck, and I wouldn't know the difference. As for the driver and a possible tattoo, I couldn't comment with any confidence. Maybe Britt had seen a bear tattoo, but maybe she'd just wanted to see one.

As we waited, the sun set, and the woods turned dark. There was no more movement by the gate. With nothing to do but sit in a dark car, I was getting drowsy and drank the second energy drink at around 10:00 p.m.

After 11:00 p.m., Brittany suggested the pickup driver lived there.

I shook my head. "He had to be let in. If he lived here, there'd be a code or a clicker."

Should I have lied? Would Britt have gone home then?

At 11:30 p.m., I wondered if the truck man was staying the night.

Midnight hit and I said, "You couldn't go back to the cabin tonight, but technically it's a new day..."

I couldn't see Britt's face in the dark, but her voice was soft. "Let's wait a little longer."

Sometime after 1:00 a.m., the conversation had dwindled into silence, and my energy drink had worn off. Catching myself nodding off, I sat up with a start. I would not be the guy who fell asleep during something that almost resembled a date. We needed a new conversation. Problem was anything I could think of to talk about was dumb or boring, and I was slipping fast. Leaning forward, I did the only thing I could think of—started pinching myself as hard as I could.

The pain helped for a few minutes, but soon my body grew used to the little yips of pain. I was sitting there with a forearm full of indents and fighting an onslaught of yawns.

Brittany's hand found my arm in the darkness, her fingers deftly feeling the marks. I could hear her smile when she asked, "Holt?"

"Yeah?" I even sounded half-asleep.

"Do you need to rest?"

"I'm fine," I muttered.

"It's pretty late. Especially for old men who go to bed at nine."

I turned to face her outline better. "I've been known to have a pumpkinizing problem," I admitted.

Brittany didn't immediately reply; when she did, she was amused. "Is that a fake medical condition?"

"I don't know about that." I yawned and shifted in my seat. "Brothers Grimm documented it hundreds of years ago. The carriage turns into a pumpkin at midnight."

Brittany placed a hand on my arm and started laughing so hard that the only sound was her gasping for air—hopefully, Brittany only found it hilarious because she was overtired.

When she was able to talk, she asked, "So the carriage turns into a pumpkin at midnight, and you...?"

Stifling another yawn, I said, "I fall asleep. Without fail, I was the first to conk out at sleepovers. Waiting for Santa, my younger sisters would always outlast me."

Britt managed not to laugh as she said, "Well, we can't stand in the way of such a serious condition. So you'd better rest up. I don't want the pumpkin to explode."

I didn't reply. I was barely awake and couldn't think of a reasonable answer. She was right. Who was I to stand in the way of science?

"If it helps," Britt said. "I promise not to put your hand in a bowl of water."

What?

Sitting up, I suddenly remembered why I was in the car. We were on a mission, tailing our possible hostage takers. I cleared my throat. "I'm your lookout."

Brittany gave my hand a squeeze. "It's okay. I release you."

Her words were like a spell. The next moment my head relaxed against the headrest, and my eyes slid shut.

"I think I see headlights."

"Mm," I said.

Somewhere far away came the sounds of a car engine turning on. Was I moving?

"Britt?" I mumbled.

"It's okay," she said. "You're safe."

There was a low rumbling mixed with the moving sensation. Britt had said I was safe. Maybe it was all a dream.

CHAPTER 7

My head was pressed against something hard and uneven. Readjusting made my neck flare. Shifting to get more comfortable, I began drifting off again when the night's adventure came to mind. Peeking an eye open, I saw that it was inappropriately bright, and all I could make out were the gray shapes of the car's interior.

"Britt?"

No answer.

Struggling to sit up, I got tangled up in the seat belt. After a brief tussle, I managed to free myself of the restraints.

"Britt?" I asked again. I reached over to the driver's seat and found it empty. Rubbing at my eyes, I managed to focus through the glare. But Britt wasn't beside me or in the back seat.

Where was she?

After I found my sunglasses, the world became slightly more bearable. I checked my phone. It had no service, but the battery was mostly charged. The clock read 9:18 a.m.

Had I really slept eight hours in the front seat of a car?

Outside the window the view had changed, and there was no longer a stone wall hidden among the trees. I was still surrounded by trees, which meant...I don't know...I was still in the forest?

Could Britt have driven back to the cabins and left me in the car when I didn't wake up? It wouldn't be the first time I'd been abandoned in a parked car. I didn't recognize the area, but maybe the Asato cabin was right out of sight. Mrs. Asato wouldn't be thrilled to spot me sleeping in Britt's car.

Trying to get out, I discovered Brittany had locked me inside—probably to protect me from ax murderers. I unlocked the door and tumbled from the car, my body all stiff and cramped.

I hoped coffee would be making an appearance soon. But after an in-depth scan through the trees, no cabin roofs or other cars were visible. Brittany's car wasn't even on the road. Had Brittany driven through the forest in the middle of the night?

"Britt!" I shouted.

The only answer I got was from a chattering squirrel.

Great.

Cartoons show little woodland pests helping people bathe and get dressed. Probably nothing more than movie magic. Still, I kept an eye on the squirrel in case he got any ideas about washing me with rabies.

Wherever I was, it was quiet. Or quiet if you didn't count all the buzzing and rustling from nature. There were no tires on pavement. No grumbling motorboats. No garbled voices drifting through the air. I didn't like it. And seriously, where was Britt? I'd been abandoned.

I yawned. Coffee wasn't happening anytime soon. This would be a rough morning. I didn't have a headache yet, but if I didn't get caffeine, it was coming for me.

Walking around the car, I found the faint mark of tires. Retracing the path Britt had driven, I came upon a narrow gravel road not too far away. From the road, I could make out the car since I was looking for it. But even in daylight, if I didn't know better, I would've missed it nestled among the trees.

"Britt!" I shouted, not that I expected a reply. There appeared to be nothing human out here.

Why had Britt left? And where could she go without her car?

The road turned in both directions, quickly vanishing into the trees. At least from this vantage, I didn't recognize any landmarks. So what happened after I fell asleep?

Checking my phone, I prayed it had miraculously gotten a signal. It had not.

In the wilderness, were there many ax murderers running around? What were my chances of running into one? Then again, what if a perfectly normal car with perfectly normal people drove by and mistook me for an ax murderer? Imagine not being rescued because I looked too creepy.

I tried to fix my hair, but what I really needed was a shower and more product. My hair was turning from wavy to curly. Having done my best to look presentable, I stood waiting beside the gravel road. Waiting, like I was expecting a bus or a taxi. Not a brilliant plan, but I'm not smart first thing in the morning.

The last thing I remembered was Britt starting the car.

Was this new destination part of her tailing mission? Or had she made a run for it? There's a chance I wasn't even in Idaho. Who knew? These could be Montanan mountains...or wherever Mount Rushmore was. Being ghosted in the wilderness was definitely in the running for our worst date—at least my head wasn't shaved.

Without caffeine, it took me a while to figure out my stand-and-wait approach wasn't working. I had a choice between following the road uphill or downhill. I chose downhill.

This was a bad morning. Had something actually happened on the stakeout? Something worth stranding an unconscious man in the wilderness?

My shoes weren't the kind meant for mountain hikes. I had some nice blisters by the time the gravel road transitioned into a dirt road and then ended in a dried-up basin that must fill with melting snow come springtime.

Seriously? Why would a road lead nowhere?

There wasn't even a good stump to rest on. I ended up perching against a jagged boulder, hoping a search party would miraculously appear. How long would I be missing before people began to look for me? Would they have any idea where to find me?

I really didn't want to walk back up the road. But the whole walk down, there hadn't even been a flicker of reception on my phone, and staying at the bottom of an abandoned road wasn't much of a plan.

My feet throbbed, and my stomach grumbled as I made the return trip. Fasting really wasn't my style. What was left in the snack bag? I tried to visualize the bag and what we'd eaten. The sandwiches and caffeine were gone, but there should be more chips and a bottle of water. Nothing like potato chips for a nutritious breakfast—they say it's the most important meal of the day.

I wasn't good at judging the distance and I kept expecting to find the car around the next bend. This went on for so long that I began to give up on finding the car. Could Brittany have returned and driven away?

A few minutes later, the car appeared, hidden in the exact same spot as before, and I felt like an idiot who still hadn't had coffee.

I was sweaty and panting from my unexpected hike, and my hair was definitely curly. While not ideal, sitting in the car with my potato chips and water was a welcome oasis. This time when I was in the car, I checked for the keys—something I should've done the first time. I also looked for some sort of note from Brittany saying, *Hey, here's why you're waking up in the wilderness...*

No luck on either front.

I did find Britt's phone, which was locked with no service. I sighed. A caffeine headache was developing quite nicely. But that headache was what pushed me back onto my blistered feet. I needed coffee.

At least I had the decency to leave a note. Granted, I mildly violated Britt's privacy by digging through her glove box to find an old receipt and abandoned pencil, but I still wrote, *Walking uphill. —H.*

As I made my way up the road, it dipped and turned. Once my phone blipped with reception for half a second, but no matter how I moved, angled, or reached, the bars never returned.

What felt like two hours later, the gravel road ended at a paved road. No cars were driving past, but pavement had to be a step closer to civilization.

Once again, I needed to choose which way to turn. I went right, but thankfully it didn't matter. My phone finally lit up with tons of notifications. Nothing from Brittany—not surprising, since her phone was still in the car.

I needed a chauffeur.

Calling Juniper brought me to her energetic voicemail. My next call was to Darren, who picked up on the third ring.

"I need a ride," I said, not bothering with a greeting.

"Where are you?" Darren asked.

"I don't know." So I hadn't thought this through.

"Are you okay?"

My only answer was to grunt.

I was tugging my hair in the middle of an unknown forest after being deserted by my almost girlfriend. No, I wasn't okay.

Since Darren had the pleasure of caffeine, he ended up talking me through how to use my phone's GPS. Not my finest moment. As it turned out, I was stuck forty minutes away from The Hive. Not ideal, but at least I wasn't abandoned in Montana.

"Okay, I'm heading out," Darren said.

"Wait!"

"Yeah?"

"Bring coffee."

Darren laughed; then the line went dead. If he didn't take the coffee order seriously, he'd be in for a very uncomfortable trip.

Sitting alone by an unused road in July was nothing like the fun vacation Brittany had promised. My feet hurt, my hair was a mess, and I couldn't decide if I should be angry or worried about Britt's disappearance.

When Darren arrived, he brought coffee and granola bars, which meant I was cranky instead of murderous.

Darren stayed quiet for the first few minutes while I drank the entire travel cup of coffee. Then he started asking questions. "What happened?"

I shrugged.

"How did you get there?"

"Car."

He tried a few more times. But since the best he got was monosyllabic answers, he gave up. I bet Darren was super thrilled he got to run this errand.

The coffee didn't make my headache go away, but I was able to think more clearly. Brittany had made a career out of helping people. What would make her leave? How was the car positioned? There weren't signs of swerving, and the car hadn't been damaged.

I really wanted an explanation. Like why she'd leave me alone in a locked car lost in the forest. Had she followed someone down there? And then what? There hadn't been any signs of a scuffle. So where was she?

The trees were packed close to the curvy road, and it was an effort to keep my eyes open. A yawn caught me off guard. It went on for so long that Darren lifted an eyebrow. He didn't comment. We both knew I was in a mood to bite his head off.

I hated that I was fighting to stay awake. Britt was out there somewhere. I shouldn't rest until I knew she was safe.

Had the car broken down? Britt may have left for help, expecting to be back before I woke up and found her gone. What if Brittany had gone to find help and stumbled upon an ax murderer?

When Darren slowed down to park at The Hive, I said, "No."

Darren's throat made an impatient sound, but he didn't comment.

"Drop me off at Britt's cabin." Then I added, "Please."

Darren knew better than to ask why and dropped me off at the Asato lodge without any further remarks.

I needed to find out if Brittany was all right. Through the whole morning's misadventure in the woods, I'd never caught sight of Britt or any traces of what happened to her. Hopefully she was safe at the cabin. If so, she had some serious explaining to do.

At the door, I remembered I was wearing yesterday's clothes and had just hiked for a few hours. I tried to smooth back my hair, but it didn't fix much. I really hoped Mrs. Asato didn't answer.

The door was opened by the short woman with dreadlocks. *Was her name Sierra or Sienna?*

My momentary relief over not facing Mrs. Asato evaporated when I saw the worry on her friend's face.

"Where's Brittany?" we asked in unison.

Britt's short friend was the first to recover. "Well, she was with you. Or she said she'd be with you. We thought she was with you."

"No, sorry." Time to get serious. I removed my sunglasses. "She was with me in the car. But I fell asleep, and when I woke up, she was gone."

This conversation had been in low tones, but then the door was flung open, and there was Mrs. Asato.

"Where is my daughter?" Her eyes were sunken like she hadn't slept much.

For some reason, I couldn't answer her. Couldn't meet her eyes. Stood there like a sweaty statue. Britt's friend with the dreadlocks put a hand on Mrs. Asato's shoulder. "He doesn't know."

At the words and the kind touch, Mrs. Asato began crying.

People needed to stop crying in front of me. I was really having a string of bad luck.

A stranger appeared and led Mrs. Asato into the adjoining sunroom, and Britt's friend brought me inside. This rental felt like a true cabin in the woods. With lots of log beams and lake-themed decor. As we walked, Sienna reminded me her name was Sienna. I reminded her my name was Holt, though I'm pretty sure she remembered.

Other women of various ages were in the cabin, and they all watched me with melancholic curiosity. The secretive glances they were sharing reminded me of Brittany's insistence she couldn't come back.

What was happening?

Sienna had me sit in a breakfast nook off a recess in the kitchen. Without asking, she gave me a fresh cup of coffee in a bear fishing mug. More coffee had me momentarily forgetting about Britt or even to say thank you.

A woman popped her head in. "She's calling the police."

"Thanks," Sienna said.

I couldn't get a good read on Sienna. It's not that she didn't seem worried, but the curious way she kept looking at me had me double-checking my collar and wishing I'd checked a mirror before coming.

I drank more coffee while Sienna watched me. Since everyone else knew what was happening, I waited for Sienna to explain. She didn't. I needed to know why everyone was walking on tiptoes and what that had to do with Britt. The problem was finding a non-rude way of asking. Finally, I threw caution to the wind. "What's going on? Am I missing something?"

Sienna gave me a sad smile. "What did Brittany tell you about this trip?"

My jaw ticked. Could someone just answer a question? This was getting ridiculous. Rubbing at my forehead, I decided to play along. "Not much. She said this happened last year, and she enjoyed it more."

"I see." Sienna refilled my coffee without saying anything else.

"Tell me." That sounded hostile. "Please."

"I wish she'd told you." The words were said more to herself than to me. Sienna sat across from me, rolling a dreadlock between her fingers. At last she said, "Fine. Britt's not here. You should know." Sienna's eyes fluttered shut. She took a deep inhale, then a long exhale. "Yesterday was the two-year anniversary of Jeremy's murder."

My jaw may have actually dropped. This trip was memorializing Britt's dead fiancé? No wonder she'd been acting strangely.

Before anything else could be said, Mrs. Asato entered, followed by The Local Sheriff. The sheriff's eyebrows shot up at finding me in this cabin, right in the middle of another mess. Last time I'd been interviewed, Britt had been sitting beside me, and now she was a missing person. Not good.

Sienna was in the best shape to give details, so she repeated to The Local Sheriff the little secret Britt had been keeping about yesterday being the two-year anniversary of her fiancé's murder.

I should have been prepared the second time through. Still, I swallowed wrong when Sienna brought up the anniversary and began cough-choking. Mrs. Asato's cold eyes only made my coughing worse.

"Last year it was healing," Sienna said, trying to get the attention back on Britt. "It was the one-year anniversary and everything was really fresh. But this time"—Sienna's eyes lingered on me—"she was ready to move on and didn't want to wallow in the past."

I nodded. Britt's spur-of-the-moment invitation made much more sense.

"Then, when we got here," Mrs. Asato cut in, "she spends half her time with a man she hardly knows."

I locked my jaw to keep my rude thoughts on the inside. This wasn't the time to start an argument with Britt's mom.

Sienna gave a few more details, and I was relatively calm when it was my turn to talk. I explained how the morning's interview with Travis led to the decision for a night mission.

Remember how I always thought stalking was a bad idea? Well, from the sneer on Mrs. Asato's face, she agreed. But I couldn't throw Brittany under the bus. For starters, our nighttime tailing was of questionable legality, and I was speaking to law enforcement. Also, even if I'd said it was Britt's idea, her mom probably wouldn't believe me.

The Local Sheriff's face had turned grim during our stories. "And how did Brittany seem? Could she have chosen to go off by herself for—"

Sienna gave a pointed head tilt toward Mrs. Asato, whose eyes were glistening with unshed tears.

"—for," the sheriff continued, "some reflection?"

I put my head in my hands. I was going to be sick.

"Brittany didn't need to reflect," Mrs. Asato said. Was she telling the sheriff or herself?

"Did you look around the car?" the sheriff asked me.

"Uh…" I shrugged. "Sort of."

"Can you show me where the car is?"

"Um." I scratched at the scruff along my chin. It had all looked alike. I didn't even know if I'd been traveling north or south…or, for that matter, east or west. Then, remembering Darren and my phone's GPS, I pulled up the info and showed the sheriff. "This is where my friend got me. I should be able to show you from there."

"Is there a spare set of keys?" the sheriff asked.

"I'll get them," Mrs. Asato said before leaving.

Once she was gone, the sheriff asked, "Did you check the car's trunk?"

"Why?" The realization that Britt might be in the trunk came a moment later. There was a strangled cry—I don't know if it was me or Sienna. Trying to regain some self-control, I tried again. "No, I didn't check the trunk."

She nodded, her face even grimmer.

The sheriff and I stood by her patrol car while Sienna put on shoes and convinced Mrs. Asato to stay behind and give her the car keys.

Sienna let me sit up front while she took the caged-in back seat.

No one said anything as the sheriff drove. Normally I prefer quiet drives, but this one dragged on and on. I was left with nothing to think about besides imagining where Britt might be. We were almost to the gravel road before I dared to ask the sheriff, "What do you think happened?"

The grimness never left the sheriff's face. "Anniversaries are hard" was all she said.

I scowled. "Why would Britt have left me in the car?"

The sheriff didn't answer.

The gravel road was easily found—according to The Local Sheriff, it was an old logging road. The sheriff quickly spotted Britt's car between the trees while I saw nothing.

Sienna and I walked slowly behind the sheriff as we approached the car.

"She wouldn't have put herself in the trunk," Sienna whispered. "This must be procedure."

"Right," I said, deciding not to mention someone else could have put Britt's body inside.

Neither of us got too close as the sheriff popped the trunk. "It's empty," she said.

I don't know how long I'd been holding my breath, but with those words, I suddenly realized my vision had been spotty. Leaning against a tree, I reminded myself to breathe. Sienna placed a hand on my shoulder, just like she had with Mrs. Asato. Thankfully, I didn't start crying. "We'll find her," she said.

I was tempted to argue. Brittany had simply vanished. Why had I let myself fall asleep? I should've known better.

"You two walk the perimeter," the sheriff instructed. She began doing different important-looking things by the car, her long braid hanging over her shoulder. Meanwhile, Sienna and I walked in ever-larger circles, searching for the merest trace of Brittany.

We turned up nothing. When the sheriff called us back, she explained with no signs of foul play and Brittany being an adult, there was nothing more we could do until the following morning.

Sienna and I were about to argue, but The Local Sheriff raised an authoritative hand. "It's already midafternoon. By the time we assembled a proper search team, it would be dark. I'll arrange everything so we can start first thing tomorrow. In the meantime, we'll hope Brittany returns after some reflection."

It was a quiet drive back but slightly less tense. When the sheriff stopped at The Hive, Sienna got out too and said she'd walk the rest of the way. She waited for the patrol car to drive away before taking a seat on a front step and letting out a sigh. "Quite a day," she said.

"Yeah."

What exactly was going on? Did Sienna plan on having a heart-to-heart, or was she going to blame me for letting Britt wander off alone? I wasn't thrilled with either option.

I sat down on the step beside her—though I wanted to march straight into the house. So far, she seemed to like me much more than Mrs. Asato did. I could survive one more conversation.

"So," she said, "the two of you were investigating?"

I scrubbed a hand across my face. "Yeah, I guess so."

When I couldn't think of anything else to say, I asked, "You're Paul's girlfriend?"

A smile flickered around her mouth. "Yes. I'm his girlfriend."

Nothing more was said, and when Sienna rested a hand on my shoulder, my breath caught. I wasn't going to start crying. There'd been more than enough of that already. But something about sitting so close to Sienna and the way her Mother Earth scent mingled naturally with the forest had caught me off guard.

"No matter what Sheriff Misty implies," Sienna said, "I know Brittany wouldn't wander off."

"Why?" I asked, an embarrassing tremor in my voice.

Sienna's brown eyes were bright. "She took the car keys with her. Brittany locked the doors to keep you safe and took the keys so she could drive back when she returned."

"But if that's true, what happened?"

Sienna shrugged. "Brittany is missing. There's not going to be a happy reason why."

This came from a woman who'd lived in Amelia's Haven for too long. Sienna wasn't used to storybook endings.

"She wouldn't have left you," Sienna said again. "Look at yourself. You're a mess."

"Thank you?" I sat up straighter and tried to fix my hair, which hadn't had any new product since yesterday morning and had gone from curly to knotty. There were also the plaid shorts and white polo I'd been wearing for thirty-plus hours.

Sienna shook her head at my attempted grooming.

"Sorry," I said. "Not all of us can roll out of bed looking perfect."

In the following silence, Sienna sighed. "Brittany was so excited you were coming," she said, almost to herself. "She'd been dreading this trip, but when you sent your booking info, she didn't stop smiling for hours. Paul asked if she was sick."

Something clenched in my gut. Was she talking about Britt in the past tense?

Sienna squeezed my shoulder. "I better go back to the cabin and give a full report. I texted there was no news, but I'm sure they'll have hundreds of questions I won't know the answers to."

I nodded, unsure if I was relieved or disappointed Sienna was leaving.

"Hang in there," Sienna said. "We'll find her."

CHAPTER 8

I stayed seated on the step and stared vacantly at the road. Chouzie greeted me with a friendly bark. His lion's mane was more majestic than usual. Had Juniper given him a blowout?

Chouzie rested his head in my lap. I idly stroked his fur while ignoring Juniper, who held his leash. My sister took the step above mine since Chouzie had taken Sienna's spot.

"A little birdie told me you had quite the adventure."

I'd never heard of Darren referred to as a little birdie—I'd prefer snitch or gossip.

When I didn't answer, Juniper poked my shoulder. "You look bad," she said.

"So I've heard," I muttered, rubbing my shoulder.

"Come on," she said, standing. "Chouzie and I were walking to town for an errand before meeting Jude for dinner."

I groaned as I hauled myself to my feet. "No. Do you have any idea how far I've already walked today?"

"It'll do you good," she promised. "I'll let you hold the leash."

"What makes you think I'd want to hold the leash?"

Juniper raised her eyebrows.

I joined them on the walk...and I held the leash. Not that I care about bonding with Chouzie. Sure he was a nice dog, but I didn't have time in my life for a celebrity.

We were almost in town when I remembered I hadn't showered or put on clean clothes. How nice of a place was the restaurant? Doubtful a restaurant in Baycliff, Idaho, had strict dress codes. Still, you never want to be the smelly guy in the restaurant.

Juniper had directions pulled up on her phone and began leading me past various businesses, all of them boasting their own Fourth of July displays. Was she buying fireworks?

"Here," she said, pointing at a bench. "You can wait here with Chouzie. He gets decision fatigue in stores."

Had my baby sister just told me to *sit* and then *stay*?

Before I could comment, Juniper had vanished into the shop, and I was left with Chouzie. The chow chow gave a low bark at a picture of a grinning poodle that was almost eye level with him on a foldout sidewalk sign.

In bold, the sign declared PROTECT YOUR PETS before giving statistics about animals running away from the sound of fireworks. The advertised solution was easy-to-attach trackers. The advertisement wasn't subtle.

Chouzie was still eyeing the reader-board poodle when I began petting him. "Someone as fancy as you must be chipped. Right, buddy?"

My hand stopped halfway down Chouzie's back. Had I just talked to a dog...in public? I half expected hidden cameras and people popping out of bushes laughing. But, for possibly the first time during the entire trip, luck was on my side, and no one saw.

When Juniper left the store, she had one item. She knelt before Chouzie and began fluffing his hair. "Are you ready to go live?" she cooed.

Chouzie gave a bark that Juniper took as a yes.

Due to an overall lack of caffeine, I hadn't pieced together the clues of what Juniper was doing until she spelled it out for her viewers.

"After the recent attempt at dognapping Chouzie, I'm taking proper precautions..." Juniper explained how she bought the top-shelf tracker that could easily be attached to any collar. If Juniper was to be believed—*granted, it's hard to believe someone peddling a dognapping theory*—the tracker was practically indestructible. Not only was the thing waterproof, but the way Juniper was talking, it had its own satellite.

I groaned and rubbed a hand over my face. Having my sister spin my break-in into a botched dognapping was one thing. But now with Britt missing, the tracker video was in very poor taste. If I opened my mouth during the live stream, none of the viewers would care about Britt and I'd be trending as #grumpybrother for sure.

"What's the matter with you?" I snapped as soon as Juniper ended the stream.

"What do you mean?"

Occasionally Juniper would purposefully annoy me so I could blow off steam. This wasn't one of those times.

"First off, we both know Chouzie wasn't the target of a dognapping. Second of all, I bet he's chipped. Third, suppose it was a dognapping attempt. In that case, it'd be someone who watches his videos, so they would know about your easily removable tracker. And finally, my girlfri—my friend is missing, and all you're worried about is social media!" I would have stormed off, but I'd forgotten to breathe during the tirade, and my vision was crowding with black dots. Chouzie barked as I sat heavily on the bench and dropped my head in my hands.

Someone sat beside me and began rubbing my back. I assumed it was Juniper—but how creepy if it'd been a stranger.

"I'm sorry," Juniper said, her voice uncharacteristically serious. "I didn't know Brittany was missing. You haven't been overly communicative. All Darren knew was you'd been stranded in the woods."

Oh. This might be an example of failing to use my words.

My anger threatened to leave, and I tried desperately to cling to it. If I stopped being mad, I'd be left with exhaustion and helplessness. I'd never cried in front of my sister, and I really didn't want to start while sitting on a bench outside a pet store with a chow chow watching.

Juniper patted my back. "Jude's waiting at the restaurant. How about we get some food?"

I sat up, leaning back against the bench. I was fighting the urge to gag at the mention of food. Who could think of eating right now? My stomach betrayed me with a loud gurgle.

"Come on." Juniper tugged me to my feet. "You must be starved. I bet you haven't eaten all day."

For the record, I'd had chips and granola bars, but Juniper wouldn't care.

Supper was a quiet affair. Jude rarely talked on a good day, I sat brooding in my chair, and for once Juniper respected the mood. Our waiter still ended up half in love with Juniper, but there was a limit to how far she could dim her personality.

Jude drove us back to The Hive, and I had to share the back seat with Chouzie. I was trying to disappear to my loft without further human interaction, but Darren was waiting in the living room to let us know The Local Sheriff had stopped by.

An official search was starting by the abandoned car at 6:30 a.m. We'd been invited to join. Juniper and Darren assured me they would help, and Jude gave a half nod—which probably meant he was coming. Then Juniper put her hand on my shoulder and said, "We'll drive you."

I probably replied. Said things to show I understood what was happening, but I needed some alone time. I had to clear my head to think properly.

Walking up two flights of stairs and a ladder took more effort than it should have, since with my workout routine, I never skip leg day. Falling face-first onto my bed, I lay completely still until my thoughts began to work themselves out. Sienna said Britt wouldn't have abandoned me in the woods without car keys.

We'd been investigating our break-in. Had she found the thugs? Had they caught her? That would mean she was either kidnapped or...or...Even in my head, I couldn't admit the alternative. Brittany had to be alive.

I'd been skeptical when Brittany had said a man with a bear tattoo had entered the Camarata estate. I thought it might be Mr. C.'s driver. Was she right? Were they the same person? Travis knew the man with the bear tattoo. Mr. Bear had used a master code to get into The Hive. He had to be one of the smiling employees on the Camarata website.

I grabbed my laptop, about to start an internet deep dive when I remembered to set an alarm for tomorrow's search party. In all likelihood, I'd fall asleep mid-investigation. Best to be prepared. I'd missed a few calls and texts from my mom. She only bugged me so much when she thought I was in trouble. But I didn't have time to discuss how Britt's disappearance was my fault.

With the alarm set, I opened my laptop and got to work. I started with the rental website. It took some scrolling to find the employee photo for Mr. C.'s driver, but when I found the face, I got the name. Scott Howard.

I then stalked him shamelessly on social media.

Problem was I had trouble finding accounts. All the photos on his Facebook page were ten years old—no bear tattoo but plenty of time to have gotten a tattoo.

Coming up empty, I moved on to Travis the Big and Scary's social media, hoping to find a pic with my bear burglar. Unfortunately, all

Travis had were pictures of him catching fish, his fiancée, and what I can only assume was a ribbon cutting for some swanky new build with Camarata Properties.

I began reviewing the other listed employees' social media profiles. Starting with men of the approximate weight and age of Mr. Bear.

I should have enlisted Juniper. This mission wasn't for the faint of heart. Going employee by employee, checking every social media site, trying to guess handles, then wading through pages of meaningless photos, all trying to find that one special man.

My vision was blurring. But it wasn't from fighting sleep. It was from staring at too many stupid pictures with happy people who didn't have missing *almost* girlfriends.

I went downstairs to get a cup of coffee. The cabin was dark. What time was it? The question was immediately forgotten once I had the mug in my hand and returned to my investigation.

The longer I worked, the more my idea seemed a bad one. Why was I wasting my night with this? Instead, I should go to the Camarata estate and convince Travis to tell me Mr. Bear's name.

Would that work? Would anyone answer the intercom in the middle of the night? For a moment I considered breaking onto the estate to find Travis. But that was crazy talk. Trespassing was exactly the sort of thing Dakota would do. And I had absolutely no similarities with that woman.

Mr. Bear probably knew something about Britt's disappearance. I had to keep searching. After exhausting my main suspects from the Camarata Properties website, I began looking at the friends and followers on the different sites.

A handle caught my attention: *@backwoodsbears*. I scrubbed at my face. Could it be so simple?

The good news was it was a public account. The bad news was the guy uploaded tons of photos. There were a lot of bear pics, and all of them were stock photos.

Then I got a shot with a face. It was Mr. C.'s driver, Scott Howard. But was Scott Howard the man who'd yelled at me to lie down on the ground?

Continuing to scroll through Scott's stuff, I made it past a couple of different girlfriends and at least three different hairstyles (one was a mullet). Then I finally found it. Posed with a beer in the back of a boat, Scott's forearm was on display, and there was that stupid bear tattoo.

Finding Scott meant there was a person I could channel all my anger on. Instead of being excited, I began deep diving into Scott Howard's life. I paid for online background checks. I got his birthday, work history, and—most importantly—his home address.

I wouldn't go *full Dakota*, but I was going to knock on the front door and ask a few questions.

As I was setting the address into my phone's GPS, my phone blared, startling me. Was that my alarm? It was still dark outside. But my phone said it was 5:30 a.m. Had I really stayed up all night? I'd never—and I do mean never—done that before.

Vaguely remembering Juniper's concern about me driving, I crept downstairs so no one would stop me. There was hardly any time to go to Scott's house and arrive on time to the search party. I couldn't waste precious minutes explaining myself.

The shower was going in the bathroom across from Darren's room, while Juniper and Jude's door was shut. There was a fresh pot of coffee, and after pouring myself a travel cup, I snuck out the front door. Keys in hand, I sighed in relief when I was on the porch steps. I hadn't seen a soul.

Then I ran into Juniper. The sky was beginning to lighten, and her silhouette was unmistakable. She popped a hip and asked, "Where are you sneaking off to?"

"What? Uh, nothing. Or...nowhere." Reminding myself I was the older brother, I switched to offense. "What are you doing out here? Keeping watch?"

Juniper's throat made the *you're an idiot* sound. "No. I'm not a prison guard. I'm taking Chouzie out before I leave him at the cabin and go hunting in the woods for Brittany."

I tried to edge past her, but Juniper wouldn't let me get away so easily.

"Where are you going?"

"You know...just running a quick errand."

"Okay."

I expected her to say more, but she didn't. She also didn't let me move past her.

"Excuse me," I tried, hoping she'd respond to politeness.

"You realize you're wearing the same clothes as two days ago?"

"So?"

"And your hair's all curly."

"Juniper, I really don't have time for this."

She laughed, but it was missing the cheery ring. "You don't see how I might find any of this concerning?"

Should I jump the guardrail? The porch wasn't too high off the ground. But would I be able to stick the landing? Right when I'd decided to jump and risk a sprained ankle, Juniper grabbed the car keys from my hand. "I'm driving."

Immediately, I began objecting. I argued it wouldn't take very long. Telling her I'd be back soon and could go with her to the woods. Anything I could think of to keep her from coming.

She ignored me, brought Chouzie inside, talked to Jude, grabbed her purse, and was in the driver's seat of my car in under two minutes.

Jude let her go to unknown locations predawn, but I needed a babysitter? It wasn't fair.

Juniper began moving the front seat and side mirrors.

"This is my car," I protested. "Just let me drive."

"Have you looked at yourself in a mirror today?"

What was she talking about?

"No," I said.

"Exactly." And with that, Juniper turned the car on.

How had she won that argument? I wasn't ready to concede defeat, but I let the matter drop. The sooner we left, the sooner I could ask Scott Howard a few friendly questions.

"Where are we going?" she asked.

"Three Seventy-One East Cedar Ridge in Baycliff." I set up my phone and started the GPS.

"And why are we going there?"

I didn't answer.

Juniper had started backing out of the driveway, but she stomped on the brakes so fast my seat belt caught me from hitting the window. "I get you have this whole sulky vibe going on, but I'm only playing Batman to your Robin if you tell me why."

"I'm Batman," I said.

"Holt!"

Smoothing back my hair, I considered my options. Juniper wouldn't move until I told her, and if I put up too much of a fight, she might get Jude and Darren involved. Then where would I be?

"His name is Scott Howard," I muttered, unwilling to make it easy for her. Unfortunately, she was patient and sat in my idling car, her face eerily similar to Mom's. "He's one of the people who broke in. I found him online by his tattoo."

Juniper's lips scrunched together like she was about to give a kiss—dumbest thinking face ever.

"Did you call Sheriff Misty?"

"No. I just found him."

We were wasting precious time. I didn't want to be late for the morning's search. But I had to talk to Scott first. Maybe he'd taken her. If he gave up where Britt was, the whole search could be called off.

Juniper put her phone on speaker as she made a call and finally reversed out of the driveway. The phone rang and rang until it went to The Local Sheriff's voicemail. There was the usual spiel about *in case of emergency call 911*, and then the voicemail clicked on. Juniper repeated what I'd said and gave Scott's address.

The Local Sheriff couldn't tell us no. Was it still too dim for Juniper to see me smirking? It was likely she was already on-site by Brittany's car and would remain out of reception until after I finished my little errand.

Scott Howard was mine.

The house was on the outskirts of town. Not close to other homes, yet not completely private. In the battle between rustic and run-down, it was definitely run-down. There were random pieces of broken machinery cluttering the ground and weeds snaking through everything. I wished it were too dark to see.

"Maybe you should stay in the car," I said.

Juniper snorted, already halfway out. "Yeah, right."

I strode to the front door and flashed Juniper my most angelic smile before pounding on the door. "Scott!" I called.

I paused to listen. Not hearing any footsteps, I continued knocking. Juniper grabbed my arm and was just getting me to stop when the door was flung open. There stood a person who was most definitely not Scott.

It was a woman a few years older than the sheriff and twice as intimidating. If Travis was *Big and Scary*, this woman was *Small and Terrifying*.

"Mrs. Howard?" I asked with my hands up. *Oh, did I mention she was pointing a shotgun?*

Her only answer was to fix the gun's aim, so it pointed directly at my chest.

"Nice to meet you." Juniper beamed, moving to my side so I was no longer blocking her from the gun. "We were hoping to speak with Scott. Is he around?"

The coldness never left Mrs. Howard's face, but the gun slightly lowered at Juniper's appearance. At the new angle, I'd be hit in the thigh. "It's early," she said. "This one here"—she jerked the gun toward me—"hasn't gone to bed yet."

How did she know?

Juniper gave a light laugh. "I'm afraid my brother's kind of rough around the edges."

The woman nodded and slowly leaned the shotgun against her wall. Could Juniper cast a spell on anyone? How had those genetics skipped me?

"I don't know where Scott is," the woman said. "That boy hasn't come home the last two nights. Not that it's unusual," she added.

Initially (when I'd pictured a face-to-face with Scott and not a shotgun), I'd planned on insisting on a look around the place to see if Brittany was there. But Scott's mom wasn't someone I wanted to mess with.

"Have you seen this woman?" I asked, showing a picture of Britt from my phone.

For a second I thought she was going to pick up the gun again and tell us to scram, but Juniper smiled, and the woman checked my phone. "No," she said. "I've never seen her."

"Okay." And with nothing more to gain, I marched to the car.

Juniper said something pleasant, thanking her for meeting with us and avoiding any references to the shotgun—all while I slammed my car door shut.

Was it time to freak out? What I really wanted to do was break some stuff, but I was in my car. All I had were the car manual and a glass water bottle. No way was I shattering glass in my car, and if I did it outside, Mrs. Howard might return with the gun.

Instead, I groaned and buckled my seat belt so violently that I pinched my fingers. "Ow," I was saying as Juniper got into the driver's seat.

"Sooo," she said, "that went well." When I didn't answer, she added, "You're welcome."

That earned a glare.

She giggled. "There's my brother."

Had I really just shown up at a stranger's home at the crack of dawn? I ran a hand through my hair as Juniper began to drive. "What am I doing?"

Juniper shrugged. "Well, now we know his name and that he's been gone for two nights."

Britt disappeared the first night Scott had. It had to be connected.

Jude had texted to let Juniper know he and Darren had left for the search. So we headed straight to the search site. It was the best option for getting there on time, but more coffee would have been good. My all-nighter was catching up with me, and the shady, windy roads made it that much harder to stay awake. I absolutely could not fall asleep. The moment my eyes shut, I'd be down for the count.

Juniper hit the gravel road just when my head had drooped against the headrest.

Right.

Sitting up, I rubbed at my eyes. Then tried to focus on finding Brittany.

Maybe Britt felt the call of nature, left the car, and fell in the dark. That theory didn't explain why she'd driven down a logging road miles away from the Camarata estate. But if it meant she was relatively okay, who cared?

There was a stream of parked vehicles leading toward Britt's abandoned car. I don't know if a lot of people was actually a good thing, but at least people had shown up. There were also dogs. Not social media dogs like Chouzie, but hard-core sniffer dogs. Could we find her?

Juniper parked, and we began the walk down to the group of searchers. "Mom texted asking about you," she said.

Oh, yeah. I'd never replied to Mom.

When I didn't answer, Juniper said, "She wants you to call. Her mom senses are tingling."

"Fine. Sure. Whatever," I said as we reached the crowd. I slipped between people to put distance between me and Juniper before she tried to push the point.

Somehow, in the shuffle of people, I ended up next to Sienna. Her dreadlocks were piled up on her head. She was ready for a day in the woods.

Looking down, I realized Juniper had been right. I was still wearing the same dumb clothes I'd put on two days ago.

Sienna smiled and gave me a quick peck on the cheek.

"Is Mrs. Asato here?" I asked, needing to say something.

Sienna shook her head. "I made her stay home." Her eyes scanned over me, searching for something. I became extra glad I'd put on sunglasses. This attention was unsettling, and I fought the urge to fix my hair. How bad had Juniper said I looked?

Instructions were given, and all the volunteers began the plodding walk between the trees, hunting for any trace of Britt. I ended up with Sienna on one side and The Local Sheriff on the other.

Whatever intense music is played during montage scenes in movies of people doing a grid search is all to hide the fact that, in reality, they're incredibly boring. Unlike the day before, this section of woods had plenty of sounds from the dogs and other searchers. Even so, the isolation of the place was unnerving.

While we'd been doing this for a long time, our slow shuffle hadn't gotten us very far. The sun was considerably higher in the sky when I spotted it. At first I thought it was litter. Some chip wrapper blown by the wind. But then I recognized the specific shade of aqua. It was Brittany's scrunchie. "Here," I called, my voice cracking.

The Local Sheriff and Sienna were instantly by my side. I pointed to Britt's scrunchie, knowing better than to touch it.

At least to my city eyes, there were no other signs Britt had been there. The landscape seemed undisturbed.

The sheriff brought the walkie-talkie to her mouth and was about to call in my discovery. Before she spoke, the radio crackled, and a voice came on the line. "We found a body."

CHAPTER 9

I was running the moment I knew where to go.

Is it Britt? Is it Britt? Is it Britt?

The words played on repeat.

Why had I wasted my time in Seattle when Britt had been in Amelia's Haven? I couldn't be too late.

There were shouts and calls as I barreled toward the body. I ignored them. Tripping, I tumbled to the ground but was back on my feet a moment later.

Is it Britt?

My lungs were screaming by the time I stumbled to the site. A tarp was already covering the body, and I tore it off, not caring a shred about procedure.

It wasn't Britt.

Suddenly my vision filled with spots. Dropping the tarp, I took a few steps away. Then I sat down rather quickly when my legs gave out. There was a rushing in my ears, and I'd never felt so sick from relief.

"Drink this." Juniper had appeared and was waving a water bottle in my face.

I don't know when Juniper or The Local Sheriff arrived, but they were both on the scene. The sheriff was standing over the body, raising the cover. When I'd looked under the tarp, all I'd seen was *not Britt*. Dinosaur bones could have been there, and all I'd known was who it wasn't. This time when the face came into view, I immediately recognized him.

"That's Scott Howard," I said.

The sheriff looked at me curiously. "And how do you know Scott?"

"Check his arm. He'll have a bear tattoo. He's one of the people who broke into The Hive."

Juniper squeezed my shoulder. "He did an internet search. We left you a voicemail."

"Ah," the sheriff said. She seemed to think something over before telling Juniper, "You should take Holt home."

Not only had the sheriff talked to Juniper like I wasn't there, but then Juniper was hauling me to my feet like I was helpless. As I was getting up, the sheriff lifted the tarp higher. There was that stupid bear tattoo, but what was more noticeable was the gunshot wound on his chest.

I may have tripped a couple of times on the way back to the car. But Juniper hovering beside me was extra. Did she really think I'd topple over any second?

"...Holt!"

What was Juniper going on about?

"Hm?"

"Are you getting in?" She was holding the passenger door open while I stood frozen beside her. I blinked, trying to remember where I was.

"I don't know why you won't let me drive," I grumbled before getting in.

It's a really good thing she didn't let me drive. I was asleep before Juniper was in the driver's seat. I woke up with my seat belt plastered across my cheek...and there's a decent chance Juniper'd had to reach around my unconscious body to put it on.

Startled, I sat up and looked around. Unbelievable. For the second day in a row, I'd woken up in an abandoned car. Sure, this time we were in the parking lot of Baycliff Grocery. Still, too soon. Way too soon.

Unlike Brittany, my sister at least sent a text saying she was making a quick food run. The message was twenty minutes old. For how small the store was, she should be back any minute.

Massaging my temples. I willed myself to become alert. It had only been an hour nap, but how could I sleep at all with Brittany missing?

Checking the store's entrance for Juniper, my eyes caught on a row of vehicles across from me—and by *vehicles*, I mean pickup trucks. But pickups of every size, style, and age. *What had I seen?* I didn't know. But my subconscious had definitely raised an alert. Looking from truck to truck, I made it through the row. Nothing.

Repeating the process more slowly, I saw a splash of faded brown between two large gray trucks. Scott's truck?

I was immediately out of the car, getting a closer look. It wasn't until I was standing in front of the truck that I realized I didn't know what I was looking for. It wasn't like I knew the license plate or remembered a specialty bumper sticker. The vehicle looked like Scott's, but it could be a random stranger's. How would I know?

The clink of metal on pavement had me turning to see a man bent over, picking up a ring of keys. His left calf was all scratched up. Didn't that mean something?

Another man joined him with a grocery bag. "Ready?" he asked. This guy had a crooked nose...

I took a step back. This was definitely Scott's truck.

The one with the crooked nose was Thug #1. I'd seen his face right before he'd covered it with a gaiter. The guy with the scratched leg had to be Thug #2. The intruder who'd tripped while running to the dock.

They walked toward me, and I couldn't stop staring.

"Can I help you?" Thug #1 asked, his voice carrying a note of menace.

Did they recognize me? I'd been facedown on the floor for most of the break-in. It didn't really matter.

I started with a strong opening. "Why are you driving Scott's truck? Did you kill him?"

"I'm borrowing—" Thug #1 was saying when he processed my second question. His mouth stayed half-open, and he looked at me like I was a raving city slicker. Maybe I was.

"Scott's not dead," Thug #2 said.

"Uh, yeah, he is."

"Uh, no, he's not," Thug #1 said.

I shook my head. This could go on all day. "What do you want—a death certificate? Someone shot him two nights ago."

Should I have said that? Were the police keeping the gunshot a secret?

"Wait. So he's actually...?" Thug #2's breath caught.

"Scott Howard?" Thug #1 asked. When I nodded, he leaned heavily against his truck.

Note to self, next time be slightly more sensitive when making a death notification.

"Why are you driving his truck?" I asked.

The thugs looked at each other, going from sad to defensive in the blink of an eye. "Scott asked us to drive his truck," the first one said.

"Just like he asked you to kill him in the middle of the woods?"

I may have gone too far.

Their stances widened before they began an ominous walk toward me. Maybe I should tone it down a bit. This whole no sleep and a missing *almost* girlfriend was getting to me.

Whether or not the thugs had murdered Scott, they'd already held me hostage once. Also, from how they were walking, they definitely had experience in fights.

"Holt, there you are." Juniper appeared beside me. Her voice was overly cheerful as she steered a cart of groceries between me and my new friends. Turning to the thugs, she gave her most radiant smile. "How are you fellows doing?"

While I personally don't understand the power my sister has over men, I can't argue with the results. A look from her had them freezing in their tracks.

"What's going on?" Juniper asked.

Thug #2 recovered enough to point a finger at me. "He accused us of something bad."

"Sorry about that." Juniper patted my shoulder. "Holt thinks he's a straight shooter, but it comes across as rude. What did he say?"

"He thinks," Thug #1 said, "that because I'm driving Scott's truck, I killed him."

Juniper gasped and swatted my shoulder. "Holt, I'm sure these gentlemen have a perfect explanation for driving Scott's truck."

I rolled my eyes. Juniper was laying it on super thick. How was it working?

"Scott asked me to drive it!" Thug #1 said. "Here, look." Tapping on his phone, he shoved the screen into Juniper's face. Since Juniper was glued to my side like a bodyguard, I also read the text from Scott dated 1:12 a.m. the night of the stakeout.

Scott: *If I stopped by your place, could you drive me somewhere and then take my truck home?*

"Perfectly reasonable," Juniper said. "Where did you drop him off?"

Thug #1 shrugged, pocketing his phone. "An old logging road. He said he was meeting someone and would get a ride back."

"And you did all that in the middle of the night?"

The man nodded.

"You're such a good friend."

Thug #1 gave such a wide grin, it showed all his teeth.

"Well, it was lovely meeting both of you," Juniper said. "Come on, Holt. Let's go." And before they knew what was happening, Juniper had returned me to the car and made me get inside while she unloaded the groceries and returned the cart.

First, Mrs. Howard with her shotgun, then the two thugs with their fists. This was getting ridiculous.

Once Juniper was in the driver's seat, I said, "You need to stop getting in the way when people are mad at me. There'll come a time when your charm isn't enough."

"You need to stop making dangerous people mad at you. And stop being an idiot," Juniper added.

"I was handling it."

"You were about to handle a punch to the face...and the groin. A simple thank-you would do."

I glared out the window the whole drive back. Once inside The Hive, I went straight to my beloved coffeepot.

"You need more sleep," Juniper said.

"I need more coffee."

"Come on," she said, tugging my arm. "You're not thinking clearly."

I rolled my eyes. "And I thought Casey was turning into Mom."

Juniper's lips pressed into a thin line. Then she tossed her hair and said, "Whatever."

Refilling my mug, I sat at the table and tried to figure out what to do. Obviously, a man getting murdered is horrible. Seeing a dead body can be traumatic. But it was so incredibly awesome the body wasn't Britt's. If saying that makes me a terrible person, so be it.

Brittany could still be alive. Had she seen what happened to Scott? Was she in hiding or possibly kidnapped for knowing too much?

It was horrendously inconvenient Scott had been killed. He'd been my best lead.

As for his buddies...well, I doubt they'd tell me anything after the downward spiral of our first interview. At least Juniper had finagled some useful information.

Why would Scott meet anyone on that abandoned road? What was he expecting? Money? Was he blackmailing someone at the Camarata estate? Also, not to be insensitive, but how did he not see the threat of being killed? It was likely whoever Scott was meeting had killed him. They'd even convinced Scott to be dropped off, so his vehicle wouldn't be on the scene. If it wasn't for Britt's disappearance, who knows if Scott's body would have been found.

It was time to pay Travis another visit. I stood up so suddenly that I collided with Juniper, who'd snuck up behind me with a plate.

"Where are my keys?" I asked.

Juniper frowned. "You're not driving like this."

"Like what?"

"Like you haven't showered in days."

"So?"

"Remember when Dad took us camping? You wouldn't stop whining about the one day you couldn't shower."

This was getting nowhere. "Keys," I repeated.

Juniper wrinkled her nose. "Nope. I'll drive."

"Whatever. Let's go."

"Eat first."

Only then did I notice the sandwich she'd been carrying. "Not hungry," I said. For once, my stomach didn't growl. Still, Juniper didn't move.

"Fine." I grabbed the plate and quickly swallowed large bites. Technically, it was supposed to be a peanut butter and jelly sandwich, but Juniper had managed to put on way too much of both, so the bread was dissolving into a gloopy mess.

How did she live like this?

After getting more coffee, I was waiting by the car when Juniper appeared with the keys and a chow chow. I ran a hand through my hair, for an insane moment valuing my car's clean interior over Britt's safety.

Chouzie grinned at me as he got into the back seat. When he sat down, I swear there was an explosion of fur and an immediate puddle of drool. I groaned but didn't comment. Juniper was acting strangely, and I didn't want her to revoke my car privileges.

Revoke my car privileges? She really was turning into Mom.

I directed Juniper to Camarata Properties. We were greeted with a locked door and a sign explaining everyone was at Mr. C.'s estate for a swanky third of July pool party in honor of Independence Day.

Who took the third of July so seriously? Was this just an excuse to light off fireworks? This was wild.

I only spoke to give directions on getting to the Camarata estate. If Juniper talked while she drove, I have no idea what she said.

How would I get past the gate? Was it time to go full Dakota?

I was supposed to be with Britt tonight for a private fireworks show. Would she be found in time for our date?

A yawn took me off guard. It went on for so long that I momentarily blacked out. That was new. I had to stay awake. If I fell asleep,
Juniper would drive in circles like I was a baby refusing to nap.

Okay, seriously, what was going on? My baby sister should never
become a mother figure in my life.

We ended up in a string of vehicles, and as we approached the estate,
Juniper was the third driver in a row to turn on her blinker for the
Camaratas' private drive. Today the gates were wide open, and our car
joined a parade of invited guests entering the party.

Inside the gates, rosebushes ran alongside the stone wall, while
perfect pine trees surrounded the winding drive. This close to my
objective, and my eyelids had grown so heavy. I bit my tongue to stay
alert since the coffee was long gone. Would the road ever end? My
eyes squeezed shut with another yawn, and when I managed to open
them, we'd broken into a clearing where the Camarata estate was on
full display.

It was one of those massive homes that had two elevators and at least
fifteen bathrooms. Following the cars past the house, Juniper parked
in a fully paved lot. Blending in with the other guests, we entered
the fenced-in yard—though calling it a yard implies a strip of grass a
teenager mows in fifteen minutes. Just like the house, the yard spared
no expense.

Off to one side were little explosions and shrieking sounds of an
endless supply of fountains, sparklers, and who knew what else. The
actual heart of the party was in and around a massive pool, complete
with a lifeguard and a water slide, looking out on a million-dollar view
of Lake Coeur d'Alene.

"We've made it," Juniper breathed before pulling out her phone
and beginning to film herself and Chouzie. The chow chow was really
in his element. Somehow looking wise and majestic, bobbing his head

politely at the many strangers who'd lined up to introduce themselves to the dog.

Whatever, Chouzie. Enjoy being beloved.

Leaving them to their new friends and followers, I began scanning the crowd for my newest nemesis—Travis the Big and Scary.

I spotted the fiancée first. The precious Camarata princess.

People got out of my way as I trudged toward her. A couple of yards away, she still hadn't noticed me. For half a second, I worried about my rumpled polo, but it was too late to change. My mouth opened to reintroduce myself when a muscular arm wrapped across my shoulder. "Hey, buddy," Travis said. "I wasn't expecting you." His voice sounded friendly enough for the casual observer. Still, the grip on my shoulder and the steel in his eyes told a different story.

Trying to go along with it, I said, "Hey, man, great party. Can we talk?"

"Sure." Travis was already steering me away from his fiancée. He punched in a code to get us into a house near the swimming pool that was way smaller than the mansion. Oh, and by *way smaller*, the house was the size of my parents' home. Was this where the staff lived? Then I read the sign, POOL HOUSE. Of course. Who doesn't have a pool house complete with three bedrooms?

Travis never let go of me until I was safely deposited on the couch inside.

Could he have taken Britt? Was she hidden in the pool house? Unlikely. Travis's face was irritated instead of worried.

"What do you want?" he asked.

"Britt," I said. Wasn't that obvious?

Confusion flashed in his eyes, but the beard hid most of his face. "You crashed one of our biggest events in the year because you're mad I didn't join a sunrise search party?"

"Scott's dead," I said.

"What?" His voice was low. His eyes darted to the door like he thought someone would barge in.

"Your buddy Scott Howard. One of the many people you know with bear or fish tattoos."

This time he understood. His shoulders slumped, and he shoved his hands into his pockets. Had I been insensitive? Since Travis wasn't about to punch me, it was a definite improvement from earlier. Still awkward. I don't recommend giving death notifications.

"Scott was..." Travis began. "Well, I knew him for a long time."

"You knew he broke in," I accused. "The moment I asked about the tattoo, you knew it was him."

Travis's only answer was to shove his hands deeper into his pockets.

Finally, I asked the million-dollar question. "What was Scott looking for?"

"I can't tell you," Travis said, beginning to pace. "Not now, not here."

"No, no, no," I said, my voice unrecognizably harsh. "Brittany's gone! This all started because of your buddy's little escapade at The Hive. Tell me why."

Travis tugged at his beard like that could bring Brittany back. Then, letting out a sigh, he looked me straight in the sunglasses. "Diamonds," he said. "My guess is someone told Scott about the diamonds."

That's what Mr. C. had been screaming about, *missing diamonds*. Made sense money would be involved in a world where the pool house was a fancy three-bedroom.

"Why was he expecting diamonds?"

Travis's face reddened, and he resumed pacing. "I love Gina" is what he finally said.

Please tell me Gina's his fiancée.

"Gina didn't even grow up here. This is just one of her daddy's many vacation homes." He shook his head. "I have no idea why she'd want to be with a simple guy like me." He sat beside me, and his eyes were pleading. "I know it's stupid, but our honeymoon is going to her daddy's villa in Morocco. I just wanted a little extra money to try to spoil her."

Rubbing my eyes, I did my best to focus. Was he making sense?

"What does your honeymoon have to do with diamonds in The Hive?"

"Right." Travis slumped onto the couch. "We're getting married on the estate. Gina's stepmom decided it would be fun if Gina and the bridesmaids all stayed at The Hive the night before the wedding and got ready there. All the dresses and jewelry were supposed to be stored there in the two weeks leading up to the wedding, so we closed the reservations. Everything was going according to plan when you messaged me."

My eyes widened as understanding began to dawn. "I told you to name your price."

Travis nodded, looking horribly guilty. "I rented the place for the list price and took the extra money."

Could I get a refund?

Not the time.

Focus.

"And all that wedding junk is here? In the pool house?"

Travis's mouth twitched. "Before I marry Gina, I'm not allowed to stay in the mansion. There's plenty of space for me and a few dresses."

"You're not supposed to see the dress before the wedding."

Wait. Had I just said that?

"Um, sorry?" Travis said.

"Who else knows?" I asked, hoping it would distract from my dress comment.

"After the break-in, Mr. Camarata was furious. Those necklaces and earrings are expensive sets and usually stored in some New York vault." Travis studied the floor. "I should have figured out sooner they'd try to steal the diamonds. Why else would they be stored in a vacant building for two weeks?"

Seeing my confusion, Travis explained. "Every year or so, my almost father-in-law has unfortunate luck. Something valuable gets stolen from a vacant property." He shook his head. "One night, late at the bar, Scott told me Mr. Camarata got him to do the robberies. All about insurance fraud." Travis shook his head. "I didn't know what to do. Gina and I were engaged. I just...I couldn't turn her father in."

Mr. Camarata was behind the robberies?

Who had Scott been visiting that night? I'd assumed it was Travis, but maybe it was Mr. C. "Did you see Scott two nights ago?"

Travis side-eyed me, and it was like a wall had gone up. "None of your business."

If it had to do with Brittany, it was absolutely my business. But pushing Travis would only work to make another person mad at me. I was learning.

"Does...?" What was her name? "Does your fiancée know the truth? About why you rented to me?"

Travis managed to look ashamed and relieved at the same time. "Yeah. I came clean after you all left." He let out another sigh. "I don't know what I was thinking. Our relationship was never about money. Though," he added, "try telling her dad that."

Just then the door opened, and Gina appeared. "Babe, have you met Chouzie?"

I swallowed a groan.

"He's a delightful little chow chow. Now I'm following him. Honestly, he might be the most famous guest at the party." She giggled. "Just don't tell Daddy."

The Chouzie monologue might have continued if her father hadn't appeared in the doorway. Mr. Camarata's clothes were expertly tailored, and I was left wondering if mine were even clean. He both noticed and decided I wasn't important in under a second.

"There you are," he said like he was talking to employees, not his daughter and her fiancé. "We're ready to make toasts but need our guests of honor."

"Of course, Daddy," Gina said. "I was tracking down my man and his new"—her nose wrinkled as she took in my haggard appearance—"friend."

They were about to leave. All three of them lived on the estate. Britt had followed someone from the estate. Was there anyone else here? If I'd been awake, I would've known who she'd seen. "How many people live here?" I blurted.

Both Gina and Mr. Camarata gave Travis a look, silently asking why I was there. Travis shrugged.

Thanks for the help, buddy.

Gina was the first person to remember her manners. She gave me a model's smile with her perfectly white teeth. "Just the three of us."

Mr. Camarata and Gina were the only people staying at the mega-mansion, while Travis was alone in the pool house?

"You're forgetting Megan," Mr. Camarata said in the bored way of the very wealthy.

"Who's that?" I asked.

Mr. Camarata gave me another uninterested look. "My wife."

Gina gave a toss of her perfect hair. "My stepmom's been gone the last week, getting some work done before the wedding."

Mr. Camarata raised one eyebrow. The only sign he was displeased. "She's taking time for herself at the spa."

Gina's perfect face almost cracked, but she said, "Of course, Daddy."

How many times would she call him *Daddy*? When Travis had mentioned *Daddy's villa*, I thought he'd been joking, not quoting.

"Oh, and Megan wants the villa in Morocco. We'll make sure the place in Hawaii is ready for your honeymoon."

Mr. Camarata left without a word of apology about changing his daughter's honeymoon plans—and people think I'm rude.

Travis closed his eyes and let out a long sigh. "Babe, I got a passport to go to Morocco because your dad said we were going to Morocco."

Meanwhile, Gina's face was as red as her father's had been in the office. "I hate when he does that."

Travis grabbed a couch cushion and smashed his face into it. "But he gets to. It's his money. He can snap his fingers and get anything he wants."

"Not this time." Gina shook her head with a look of determination she also got from her father. "He told us Morocco. We're going to Morocco."

Travis made a face. "I don't want to be honeymooning with your dad and stepmom. Hawaii should be fun. It's a shorter flight."

If possible, Gina's face turned redder. "Hawaii is where basic people go to honeymoon!"

Whoa.

I may have said that out loud. At any rate, that was when they remembered they had an audience.

"You should go," Travis said, hoisting me to my feet.

"Yeah, um..." Should I say congratulations? I settled on "Thank you for your time."

"Right." Travis slung an arm over my shoulder and walked me through the party to the parking lot. "Where's your car?"

Pointing, I said, "Over there." This could be the sleep deprivation talking, but I found Travis personally escorting me off the property hilarious. What did he think I'd do?

Travis began walking us in that direction when I stopped him. "I don't have the keys. The woman with the chow chow has them."

He may have muttered something, but his beard hid the movement. "Stay" was the only word I heard.

Why was everyone treating me like I was a dog or a baby?

Travis forced his way through the group of people surrounding Juniper and Chouzie. He spoke into Juniper's ear, and soon enough, the trio was returning to the spot where I'd stayed like an obedient dog-baby.

Eyeing me, Travis decided not to take me by the shoulder again. Juniper kept up a cheerful stream of chatter as Travis watched us load up into the car.

"Happy Fourth," I called.

"Yeah," Travis said, shoving his hands into his pockets.

Travis didn't move from his place in the parking lot as Juniper backed out and pulled away. Would he spend the rest of the party standing there making sure I didn't return?

Juniper smiled. "Thanks, Holt, for being a party crasher. That was some excellent networking."

"Mm-hmm."

I settled back in the chair, reminding myself not to close my eyes. I almost smiled. I'd been in the pool house with the person who'd killed Scott Howard and hopefully taken Britt. I just needed to figure out who that was.

CHAPTER 10

Jude's car was in the driveway when we got back to The Hive. Jude and Darren were lounging on the uncomfortable couch, and the TV had pseudo-famous actors on the screen. At our entrance, Jude began playing on his phone, and Darren paused the show.

"Where've you been?" I asked.

Darren jumped up and joined us. "Are you kidding?" When I didn't answer, he asked Juniper, "Is he kidding?"

She shook her head.

Darren gave me a once-over before mouthing, *Wow*, and going to the kitchen.

"What's up with him?"

For once Juniper didn't answer. Instead, Jude said without looking up from his phone, "We spent the entire day in the woods trying to find a trace of your girlfriend, and you didn't remember where we were."

"Oh." So I was a jerk. "Wait"—I turned to Juniper—"should we have stayed?"

Juniper shook her head. "You had to leave."

I was tempted to argue. But since I'd almost fainted at the sight of a dead body, I decided to drop it.

"I take it Holt's not cooking," Darren called from the kitchen.

"Definitely not," Juniper said.

Where had that come from? "I'm a good cook."

Juniper scrunched up her face. "You haven't exactly been paying attention to detail."

What did that mean?

To prove them all wrong, I tried to help Darren in the kitchen. But it didn't go well. He wouldn't let me chop the peppers and positively freaked out when I got *too close* to the burner. I really was being treated like a child. In the end, all I was *allowed* to do was sit and watch from the table. Was this how my nephew felt in time-out?

I should concentrate on Scott's murder and who took Brittany. But focusing on details was difficult. For some reason, my brain was all muddled.

According to Travis, no one else knew he'd rented me The Hive. Scott had expected to waltz in, take the diamonds, and leave.

It was an open secret Mr. C. stole from himself to commit insurance fraud. Presumably, he'd been the one to send Scott. But if that were true, why had he yelled at Travis about the diamonds the next day? Scott would have updated him that night, so Mr. C. would have confronted Travis that night.

And while Scott may not have been a law-abiding citizen, I don't know why he'd be murdered.

As for suspects, there was Travis. But he'd come clean to his fiancée and told his almost father-in-law a convincing lie. Besides, it's not like he would have hired Scott to steal diamonds he knew were in the pool house. With Gina, I could make up any number of motives, from having an affair with Scott or trying to prove herself to *Daddy*. Then, Mr. Camarata was an all-round jerk. If Scott was letting secrets slip in barrooms, Mr. C. might have decided he was a liability.

"Are you going to eat?" Darren asked.

Huh? Refocusing, I realized there was a plate of food in front of me, and the other three were at the table.

"Um, yeah."

Darren's cooking wasn't anything special, but it was better than the gooey mess Juniper had fed me. After the meal, Darren said to leave the dishes on the table. He wanted to tell everyone what happened during the search. Why hadn't he told us while we ate?

They all went to the living room, so I followed. I'd just found a semi-comfortable spot on the couch when Juniper scooped up Chouzie and set him beside me. After giving me a soulful look, Chouzie rested his head in my lap. His breathing first grew rhythmic, then became low snores. Could I be annoyed at Juniper while not wanting Chouzie to leave?

Ugh. Had I become a Chouzie fan?

"It really started," Darren was saying, "when Jude and I were figuring out who would drive. While I'd already driven there..."

Yawning, I sat back. Darren was usually good at telling stories. This one was rather slow and plodding.

"...since he's more comfortable on curvy roads..."

A distant firework had Chouzie jumping up and barking. Grunting, I sat up.

Where am I?

"Chouzie, walk." Jude had Chouzie leashed and out the door in a matter of seconds.

Why was I on the couch? There was work to do. If I typed up everything that happened on my laptop, I could put my thoughts in order.

"Holt," Darren said as I stood up. "Story's not over."

Right. I sat back down. Not that I was interested. The story was frightfully boring, and I hadn't heard most of it. Darren picked up where he'd stopped, apparently mid-botany lecture, explaining the plants he saw and the odors they emitted. His voice grew farther and farther away...

Then a pounding on the door had me lurching up. When had I closed my eyes?

"This close," Darren said to Juniper on his way to the door.

What was he talking about?

"Evening, Sheriff," Darren said.

The Local Sheriff stood grimly in the doorway, her long braid hanging over one shoulder. My stomach clenched with dread. She wasn't here with good news.

"Did you find Brittany?" Juniper asked when I didn't speak.

"Ms. Asato is still a missing person," the sheriff said, not quite meeting Juniper's eyes.

"Then why are you here?" I asked.

"Mr. Jacobs, we'd like you to come to the station for some additional questions."

It took me a moment to understand the implication. "I'm a suspect?"

"Holt, don't say anything." Darren blocked the door with his body, breaking our eyeline. "Is he under arrest?"

"No." The sheriff's voice was hard. "We just want an official interview."

"Right," Darren said. "The kind with mics and video cameras. My client respectfully declines."

Have I mentioned Darren's a lawyer? He's a lawyer. Though I don't remember him doing criminal law.

Darren and the sheriff began talking in hushed tones. Which I hated. I got closer to be part of the action. The moment I appeared, The

Local Sheriff ignored Darren completely. "Holt, it's a few questions. We just want to find Brittany."

That last sentence hung in the air.

"I'll go," I said.

Darren's hand clamped down on my shoulder. "Excuse us for a moment. I need to confer with my client." He shut the door in the sheriff's face and then began dragging me through the living room.

I groaned. I'm over six feet tall and in good shape. People needed to stop hauling me around.

Darren didn't say a word until we were safely in the kitchen. Juniper had followed and was hovering by the fridge. "Holt," he said, looking me full in the eye. "I need you to focus. This is a bad idea."

I shrugged. "It's just a couple of questions."

"Holt."

Why did he keep saying my name?

"Think about it," Darren continued. "You were the last person to see Brittany, and your only alibi is sleeping."

"I was sleeping!"

Darren patted my back in a way that was supposed to be soothing. "I know that. Juniper knows that. But the police don't know that. If you go in there, they'll ask you the same questions over and over again, trying to catch you in a lie."

For a moment, I considered what he was saying. Of course I was a suspect. If I hadn't been so worried about Brittany being missing, I'd have realized it sooner. Could I really go to jail over this? All I wanted was her safe return.

"No." I took a step back. "Sorry, Darren. I have to go. If they think I took her, they won't explore other options. I need to clear my name so they find the real culprit."

"Holt." Darren's voice cracked. "Please."

I shook my head and walked away.

Juniper grabbed my hand as I left the kitchen and said, "I love you."

I rolled my eyes. "Come on, guys. I'm not getting hanged." I was about to leave when I added to Juniper, "But I love you too."

At the front door, Darren caught up to me. "Wait." Grabbing his wallet and keys from a side table, he joined me. I was about to argue, but Darren raised a hand. "I'm not letting you do this by yourself."

Yes, sir.

The Local Sheriff was waiting on the porch, and Darren spoke before I could. "I'll drive my client to the station."

On the ride over, Darren did everything he could to talk me out of the interview. When that didn't work, he tried to convince me to have him do all the talking. It was well meaning but a waste of breath. I hadn't kidnapped Brittany. Hopefully, the police would see that. They wouldn't move past suspecting me until I'd answered all their questions.

Brittany was alive. Her body hadn't been found near Scott's. She had to be alive. I would do anything to bring her back. And Darren could deal with it.

It wasn't until I was seated on a chair bolted to the floor by a metal table that I remembered I was running on coffee fumes. Also, to be petty, I'd pictured a fancy interrogation room like on TV. The reality was a room designed in the eighties with flickering fluorescent lights and the smell of urine.

Don't be rude. Be respectful. Don't mouth off.

I was doomed.

The sheriff was joined by an equally stern colleague with a droopy mustache. Their opening questions were almost casual. The sort an acquaintance might ask at a college reunion.

I repeated the broad details of the break-in and our stakeout. Next, they started getting specific. Stuff like *What time did this happen?* and *Who else was there?*

The flickering light and bombardment of questions left me with a horrible headache. Occasionally, Darren would interject when they asked the same question one too many times. There was something different about him and the way he spoke. I'd never seen him like that. It was almost scary.

Then the interview went downhill. Rather abruptly and very quickly.

An evidence bag was set on the table with the aqua scrunchie inside. "Do you remember this?"

"Britt's scrunchie? The one I found this morning? Yeah, I remember it."

Darren's throat made a displeased sound.

The Local Sheriff said, "We had a tip that you may have planted it in the woods."

What?

Why would I do that?

Who even knew I found it? It'd been discovered right before Scott's body was found, which was the day's big news. The only people around me were The Local Sheriff and Sienna.

Sienna? I thought she liked me. Had she really accused me of planting evidence? That didn't seem right. But Sienna wasn't alone. She would have gone home and told Britt's mom everything that happened...

"Wait, did Mrs. Asato call the cops on me?"

The cops didn't answer, but their eyes gave them away.

I turned to Darren. "She hates me. Britt's mom hates me."

Darren's mouth twitched. I'd just been accused of planting evidence, and I was worried about what Britt's mom thought of me.

"Mr. Jacobs." The sheriff tried again, picking up the evidence bag. "Did you plant this?"

"Of course not."

I sighed. They weren't moving past me as a suspect. It was ridiculous that anyone would think I could hurt Britt.

"This is so messed up," I said. "Can't you just find the real culprit?" It was getting harder to concentrate on the questions and harder to form sentences to answer with. So I let something slip. Something that wrinkled Darren's forehead. "Scott's buddies are the ones that broke in. They even have his truck."

Darren squeezed my arm. The officers exchanged glances.

"Excuse me?" The Local Sheriff asked.

Closing my eyes, I tried to massage the tension from my temples.

"Who has Scott's truck?" she asked again.

Darren's grip on my arm tightened.

"I don't know their names," I said. "Scott's buddies. The thugs. One has a crooked nose, and the other has cuts along their leg. They were at the grocery store."

The cops began murmuring to each other.

I shook my head. "Must I do everything?"

"Holt, shut up!"

Lawyer Darren is mean.

The droopy-mustache cop left the room while The Local Sheriff asked, "Why didn't you call the police after you saw them?"

"Um..." I was floundering. Saying *I hadn't thought of it* sounded dumb.

"How do you know what Scott's truck looks like?"

They really weren't moving past me as a suspect. At the cabin, The Local Sheriff had said I wasn't under arrest. Was that still true?

"Can we go?" I whispered to Darren.

For the first time all night, Darren almost looked happy. He stood. "That's enough questions for this evening. If you need any follow-up information, feel free to reach out over email." Darren slid an embossed business card across the table.

The Local Sheriff picked it up gingerly, like it was infected.

"Don't leave town," she said.

The smile Darren shot her was venomous. "My client is here on vacation. Once his vacation is over, he has commitments to return to in Seattle." He gave a professional nod. "You understand." Darren held the interrogation door open for me, and we left the station.

Darren didn't say anything as he started the car and drove away. Even in the darkness, I could see how rigid Darren's posture was. I waited for him to speak. At one point Darren said, "Holt..." before going silent.

My eyes were half-closed when a red explosion of a firework through the trees had me sitting up.

"Wait," I said. "That story you were telling, it was boring on purpose. You wanted me to fall asleep."

"Yeah, congratulations." Darren's tone was dry. "You figured it out. And it only took you two hours." Darren drummed his fingers on the steering wheel before saying, "I know you want to find Brittany, but you'll have a better chance of figuring out what happened if you get some sleep."

I didn't have an answer for him. Me sleeping is what got us into this mess.

When we'd parked by The Hive, with the cabin glowing from the lights Juniper and Jude had on, Darren said, "This is really serious."

I'd gotten distracted by how clearly I could see Juniper and Jude. The Hive really was a fishbowl.

"Holt?"

I shrugged. My focus couldn't be saving my own butt. It had to be finding Britt.

Darren sighed. Had he read my thoughts? When he didn't say anything else, I went into the cabin. Chouzie ran up and licked me. Juniper was waiting with a thousand questions, and even Jude set down his phone at my entrance.

After putting together the most basic answers, I disappeared upstairs the moment Darren appeared to distract Juniper. Though I don't think he could tell her anything since he was my lawyer...Then again, was he really my lawyer if I hadn't paid him? Yet another question that didn't matter in light of Britt's disappearance.

I climbed the two flights of stairs and went up the ladder, forgetting the ceiling on the fourth floor was too low and banging my head when I straightened. I made it to my bed, muttering my frustration, then sat on the mattress with my legs stretched out and opened my computer. Time to type everything I knew.

The Local Sheriff originally implied Brittany might have chosen to disappear. But where could she have gone without her car? She wasn't in the woods. They'd been thoroughly searched by people and sniffer dogs. The only sign she'd been there was the scrunchie that the police (or Mrs. Asato) thought I'd planted.

There it was, lying on the ground in front of me. Could Sienna have planted it? What reason could she have? Unless Britt had chosen to vanish and gotten Sienna to help. But why?

This didn't explain who killed Scott or why he'd bothered to break into my cabin looking for diamonds. What if Brittany had followed him out there and killed him? Then Brittany got Sienna to help her make a run for it.

I rubbed at my face.

For the second time in two months, I'd suspected Brittany of being a murderer. What was the matter with me? Maybe I did need sleep.

This was going nowhere.

Choosing a new angle, I began charting Scott's movements. First he'd broken into our cabin. The next day he'd gone to the Camarata estate and was killed either late that night or early the following morning.

Yawning, I scrubbed at my eyes and tried to blink the fuzziness away. What had Britt seen that night? Whoever killed Scott must've taken her. Perhaps they were more squeamish about killing innocent bystanders. If that were the case, how long would they keep Britt captive?

Unbidden, Brittany, trying not to laugh when I needed the burner of onions turned off, popped into my head. There was nothing better than making her laugh. If we found her and if she let me, I'd make her laugh all the time.

What was the point of Seattle? It had the reputation of being the "Emerald City," but the only way it attained that level of greenness was by being gray and drizzly all day, every day.

It was so inconvenient Scott was murdered on the same day as Britt's fiancé. On any other night, she wouldn't have been stalking strangers through the woods.

All the suspects working for a rental company were also very unfortunate for Britt's sake. Because where would someone with unlimited properties hide a kidnapped person?

Really not a fan of Camarata Properties. I should leave them a very bad review.

A hand on my shoulder had me screaming and leaping out of bed, only to bang my forehead on the ceiling.

"Juniper?" I groaned.

Strangely, she didn't laugh at this display of bravery. "Mom called me," she said.

"What? No." Rubbing at my forehead, I tried to figure out if there was swelling. "What did you tell her?"

Juniper sat on my bed, behaving annoyingly Mom-ish. "She saw online the news about Brittany's disappearance. She's worried, and you haven't answered any of her texts or calls for the past two days."

"It's online?"

"*Murdered body found in the woods* and a *missing woman*? Yeah, it's online." Juniper shrugged. "So far there's not that much coverage, but it could explode."

I frowned. Had Mom been texting? I couldn't remember. Shrugging, I said, "Well, if she's talked to you, then she knows I'm alive."

"Holt." Juniper waited for me to meet her eyes. "She's threatening to come up here."

I wanted to start pacing but didn't want to hit my head again. "No! No. She can't. They're moving to Australia."

"Not for another week."

Hold on.

I sat down suddenly. Juniper's comment about a week meant something. What was happening in a week?

Juniper had continued talking, but I was too busy trying to remember why a week was important. Then she shook me.

"What?"

"You need sleep."

I frowned. "There isn't time."

Juniper scrunched her nose. "Look, I told Mom not to worry. Everything was under control. But"—she waved a finger in my face—"if I call her back and explain how you haven't changed your clothes or showered in days and that your hair's a..." She gestured toward my head since apparently there were no words. Her tone then went suspiciously sympathetic. "I know you're worried about Brittany. But you won't figure anything out when you're too tired to take a shower."

Running both hands through my hair, I attempted to fix whatever problem had her so worried. Resting my head in my hand, I was surprised by how much scruff I felt. I'd been known to have some vacation stubble, but what I felt was rough, with absolutely no grooming.

I sighed. Juniper possibly being right is one of the worst things in the world.

When Juniper left a little later, she had all my electronics. I was lying down with the lights off and was supposedly going to drop off into immediate sleep.

But it didn't matter if my eyes were closed or open. I couldn't relax. What did Mom and Dad leaving for Australia in a week have to do with Brittany?

CHAPTER 11

Juniper had forgotten about the fireworks. It was the third of July. One of Britt's two magical days where you could shoot fire into the sky and the area echoed with explosions. Not only was it loud, but every firework was a reminder I was supposed to be at the lake lighting them off with Brittany.

I thought they were only allowed during certain hours. Without my tech, I didn't know what time it was, but it felt pretty late. Still, with the police busy trying to arrest me for a murder and a missing person, they might not have the time to go from cabin to cabin telling people to stop.

The couple of times I started to doze off, a mortar would explode. This was immediately followed by Chouzie's ferocious howls. When the clamor died, I'd been lying in bed too long to fall asleep.

One week...one week...

My parents were going to Australia in a week. Travis and Gina were getting married in around a week. Then what? A honeymoon to Hawaii. Originally they were going to Morocco. Which was a different country.

I sat up.

Someone had killed Scott and kidnapped Brittany. Was the plan to release Brittany after the wedding? Britt's testimony would be worthless if the killer was unreachable. All they'd need was a good getaway.

Did Morocco have an extradition treaty? Reaching for my phone, I realized my mistake. Juniper had it. How was I supposed to look up Morocco when I didn't have the internet?

This was the worst.

Mr. C., Gina, and Travis all wanted to go to Morocco. But who wanted it as a vacation, and who needed it as a getaway? I had to figure out who that was.

If I went to the sheriff, she'd think I was making up stories to save my own skin. I had to do this by myself.

I did my best to sneak down the ladder and the first flight of stairs. I held my breath as I reached the landing, worried I'd meet Juniper with her arms crossed and hip popped.

She wasn't there. I tiptoed past the master bedroom before slipping downstairs. I was nearly to the main floor when movement and heavy breathing had me swallowing a scream and falling back into a seat on the steps. A moment later, Chouzie's majestic face was pressed up against mine.

"Hey, buddy," I said, relief washing over me. It was a dog, not an intruder or my brother-in-law who was secretly James Bond. I began petting his hair. Chouzie moved, and my fingers got tangled against something on his collar. Juniper's tracker pressed into my palm.

Huh. Juniper had my tech. If I got into too much trouble, I'd be unable to call for help. Also, no one could find me without my phone's tracking software. But I had the next best thing at my fingertips.

Ruffling Chouzie's fur, I considered my options. First off, no matter what Juniper said, no one was trying to dognap Chouzie. Secondly, he was definitely chipped. And to circle back to reason number one, anyone trying to dognap Chouzie would already know about Juniper's tracker via social media and just remove it. It's not like I'd be putting Chouzie at risk.

"Sorry, boy," I whispered as I removed the tracker and put it in my pocket.

My idea was half-baked, but it was the only one I had. After taking the tracker, I not only felt guilty but also anxious. Juniper could appear at any second. Quickly filling a thermos with coffee, I found a notepad in one of the kitchen drawers and scrawled a note.

Gone fishing. —H.

P.S. Check Chouzie's tracker.

I debated signing off with a row of x's and o's. In the end, I chose not to and left the note by the coffee maker.

Finally, I needed car keys. A quick search for my keys came up empty. Juniper must have the keys with my phone and computer in her bedroom. But while my keys may have been hidden, Darren's were lying on a side table. As beautiful an invitation to borrow someone's car as I've ever seen—Darren's so trusting.

Unlocking the front door, I slipped outside. It wasn't even sunrise, and already I'd managed to steal from a dog and commit grand theft auto. I have no idea why Juniper accused me of being too tired to think clearly.

There's a chance I got lost on my drive to the Camarata estate. But it had nothing to do with being exhausted. I'd never driven there. It had always been Brittany or Juniper. And who can see anything in the dark?

After a few U-turns, I made it to the iron gates of the Camarata estate. I drove past and parked in the spot Brittany had chosen the other night.

Time to go full Dakota.

Climbing over a rock wall is harder than it looks. Sure, a professional rock climber could do it in the blink of an eye. However, I'd chosen a career that paid money, so I kept falling. The wall wasn't even that high. If someone could give me a boost, I'd make it over no problem. Too bad everyone I knew thought I was incompetent.

I tried going rock by rock. Sucking in my already flat and muscular stomach. Then going barefoot, in case I got a better grip.

Nothing worked.

Once I made it up four feet and almost reached the top, then everything tipped, and I fell onto moss and pine needles.

I kept trying different methods until I was worn out, and my arms were full of little scratches. Taking a break, I was leaning against Darren's car, wishing I could get a hand up when I realized I'd been an idiot. Maneuvering the vehicle through a few trees, I lined it up with the wall.

Very proud of myself, I climbed up the hood, then onto the car's roof, before scrambling up to the top of the wall.

Genius.

I was absolutely great. Step aside, Jude. I'm the American James Bond. I could start doing rescue missions as a side job. Or teach classes, sharing how to adapt to different emergencies. I could even give a TED Talk. Truly, there would be no end to the accolades.

I lowered myself down the other side and hung suspended for a few seconds. The sky was beginning to lighten, but it was well before sunrise, and I couldn't tell how far away the ground was. Then, reminding myself Juniper was wrong and I was awesome, I dropped down and landed with a thud in a thicket of rosebushes.

I gasped as thorns traced patterns up my calves. In my panic to get out, I didn't walk out of the perimeter but kept trudging through the vicious bushes.

Then I thought of the tracker. Had it fallen out in my tumble? The thought sobered me enough to check my pockets. It was still there, and that small task calmed me enough to find a way out. I made my escape, at last free to snoop around the estate.

My half-baked plan had heated up from *stealing Chouzie's tracker* and *breaking into the Camarata estate* to include *getting kidnapped.*

It was brilliant. How had it taken me so long to come up with it? If I got kidnapped, they would bring me to where Brittany had already been kidnapped. I would find her, and we would share an epic first kiss as fireworks exploded over the lake.

What is the best way to be kidnapped by a murderer? On the one hand, I needed my prowling to be obvious enough that someone with a guilty conscience would spot me while not so obvious anyone else would notice and call The Local Sheriff—Darren would love to explain my trespassing.

Light was brightening the sky, but I used the lingering shadows to pretend to search for Britt. There were plenty of outbuildings near the mansion that could hide a person. Not that any of my suspects were stupid enough to do that.

I'd peered into the windows of the garage and gardening shed when a sound had me ducking down. The door to the pool house opened. Gina and Travis appeared. After a hug and a long goodbye kiss, Gina jogged from across the lawn to the main house. Travis stood at the entrance watching and gave her a wave before they both entered their respective homes.

My heartbeat picked up, and I could feel its rhythm in my ears. Had they seen me?

A door clicked from the second floor of the mansion, and I saw Mr. Camarata's retreating figure through the glass. He'd been watching Gina and Travis, but had he seen me?

Would someone come and get me?

Not wanting my role as a sitting duck to be overly obvious, I took the path down to the water and searched the boathouse. At any second I expected to be held up at gunpoint. I wanted it to be Mr. Camarata. It'd be awesome to wipe that smug smile off his face...assuming everything went according to my awesome plan.

The boathouse was open, but the boat and cabinets were locked. I didn't fiddle with the locks. It's not like they'd hidden Brittany on a shelf.

The speedboat rocking on its mooring captivated me. Had Brittany been here? Could I have The Local Sheriff dust for fingerprints? Could I call? How would that conversation go? *Hey, so while I was trespassing, hoping to be kidnapped, I saw the Camaratas' boat and thought you should check it out...No, I don't have any actual proof the Camaratas took her or that she was ever in the craft.*

The boat bumped against the dock, and I blinked. Shaking myself, I decided to leave the boathouse. If the fireworks last night were any indication, Lake Coeur d'Alene took the Fourth of July very seriously. If I stuck around too much longer, I'd run into Mr. Camarata's new wife and a group of her friends on their way for a day on the water...assuming Mrs. C. was done getting plastic surgery.

I yawned. I should go. Once Darren woke up, he'd be pretty antsy about his car. It's not fair. Brittany could accidentally get kidnapped, whereas I was positively advertising for a chance and no takers.

Exiting the boathouse, I hadn't taken two steps when the barrel of a gun was pressed into my back. For a single moment, I couldn't stop my smile. It had worked.

"Why are you here?" It was a woman's voice, which could only mean Gina.

I held up my hands and turned around slowly. She stood, gun in hand, watching me nervously. I wasn't going to try anything. Hopefully, she could tell I just wanted one thing.

"Where's Brittany?" I asked.

Gina made a face like she was bored. "Who?"

"Take me to her." That sounded more desperate than intended.

She smirked, and I pictured her with a broken nose.

Sensing the change, she took a step back while holding the gun a little higher. "You're trespassing before sunrise. What do you think happens to me if I kill you in self-defense?"

Huh. You know, I hadn't thought it all through.

Under these circumstances, she could confess to killing me and not even be slapped on the wrist.

"Look at you," Gina said, using the gun to gesture along my body. "You're practically a rabid animal. Everyone would believe I feared for my safety."

Had she implied I had rabies? That crossed a line.

"That's a nice gun," I said—not that I noticed anything beyond the barrel. "Is that the same gun you used on Scott?"

It was barely visible in the early-morning light, but Gina flinched.

I grinned. "The police would find out the shots came from the same gun. They might even search the surrounding area and find out who's been on your boat."

Her eyes tightened, and my shoulders relaxed. Britt had been in the boat. I had felt her presence.

"Who knows you're here?" she asked.

I held my hands up even higher. "No one."

She gave me a long look before deciding I was telling the truth. "Well, in that case, allow me the honor of calling Sheriff Misty and letting her take you away."

What? It wasn't supposed to go this way. Gina held the gun in one hand as she pulled out her phone.

"Take me to Brittany!"

She shook her head and began punching in numbers.

"The gun. Your gun. I know about the gun."

Her voice turned childish. "What gun? I don't have any guns."

How was this happening?

Think, Holt, think.

"I can prove it!"

Her thumb hovered above the call button.

Good news, I had her attention. Bad news, I was mostly bluffing.

"I know all about it," I continued, trying to remember any little detail that might be useful. "You're not opposed to honeymooning in Hawaii because it's where *basic people* go. You care about leaving the country because you're a kidnapping murderer."

Gina's face flushed and contorted. "Hawaii is for basic people."

Seriously? Hawaii was the part she needed clarified?

"Besides," Gina said, "Scott did little jobs for Daddy all the time. If Daddy could bend the rules from time to time for a little untraceable cash, why couldn't I? So I asked Scott to steal the diamonds. It was convenient since"—she gave a little laugh—"I hated those diamonds. The patterns were so tacky. Megan picked them out. Said it was her duty as a stepmom to choose the wedding jewelry."

She stopped talking, and I realized I was supposed to say something. "Um, okay."

That was all she needed. "Everyone got so mad. Scott was mad that you were there. Daddy was mad Travis hadn't mentioned The Hive was rented. Daddy was also mad at Scott for breaking in without his permission. So Scott told Daddy I'd made him. When Daddy heard it was my idea, he said it was fine and wrote me a check for what the diamonds were worth. But then Scott still wanted his cut and threatened to tell Travis that I was just like Daddy."

"And you're not?"

My tone may have been dripping with sarcasm.

"Of course I'm not like Daddy! I'm a good person. Travis needs to think I'm a good person." She took a step closer. "Scott was going to ruin it."

"And Brittany?"

"Get in the boat, and you'll see."

I positively ran to the boat. Gina was slower to follow. First she unlocked one of the cabinets, then grabbed a handful of zip ties. Gina eyed me, the boat wheel, her gun, and the zip ties.

"I won't try anything. Promise."

She decided to trust me enough to put the gun down and zip-tie me. When it came to tying me up, Gina went overboard. My arms and legs were bound together multiple times, and there were even cords attaching me to the boat (like I'd be tempted to swim without the use of my arms or legs).

I was positioned awkwardly, semi-reclined on the seat. The engine turned over, and soon wind was whipping across my face. Guess I was one of those fancy people who rode speedboats on Independence Day.

Craning my head, I watched as we flew across the water. Minutes went by, and we were heading toward a wilder, almost abandoned stretch of cliffs. Gina twisted the wheel until we were heading straight for a craggy cliff. At first I wasn't worried, but as Gina neared the rocks without any sign of slowing, I began to squirm. Was she going to drive us into the rocks?

I was bracing for impact when she cut the main engine, and we putted slowly through a narrow passage of rocks invisible from the rest of the water. The boat turned into an enclosure of Batcave levels of secrecy. There was a small stretch of land surrounded by cliffs and water with a dilapidated cabin in the center.

Gina pulled the boat up beside an old rickety dock and tied it off. She was way too pleased with herself, like having a secret hideout wasn't a major cliché for villains and seven-year-olds alike.

She cut off all the zip ties binding my legs and the ones attaching me to the boat but left the ones she'd put on my wrists and arms.

"Out," she ordered.

I eyed the dock suspiciously. Could it hold my weight? If I fell into the water, Gina wouldn't rescue me. How deep was the lake here? We were close to shore, but I couldn't see the bottom.

"Get out," Gina repeated, this time waving the gun.

Fine. Whatever. I'd been a lifeguard at a public pool. I could teeter above murky water of unknown depths with my hands bound.

Scrambling out of the boat was not my most graceful moment. Not only were my arms wrapped together, but the zip ties were so tight, my hands were numb and tingly. Gingerly rolling over the boat's edge, I kicked my legs around until they connected with the dock. There was a light splash as something fell from my pocket. Were those Darren's keys? If Gina didn't kill me, Darren would. The wood beneath me shifted and groaned when I put my full weight on the dock. Needless to say, I got off that OSHA violation as quickly as my legs would carry me.

Gina came on land more sedately, with her gun half-raised. I wasn't trying to escape. I just needed to find Brittany.

She directed me up past the cabin. There was a small upright building that I assume was an outhouse, the wood moldy and sagging to one side.

"Get in," she said.

Nausea tickled the back of my throat. One person could barely fit in there, let alone two. "Britt?" I asked as I tried opening the warped door.

"What are you doing?" Her tone was impatient. "Not there. Here."

Oh. A shed. So much better.

Under normal circumstances, I would have refused to get into the shed Gina was standing beside. But while the structure looked like a sudden wind would knock it over, it could easily fit two people and would be less revolting than hanging out in an abandoned outhouse.

Gina kept one eye on me as she unlocked the padlock and unwound the chains holding the door shut. "You have a guest," she called before opening the door just enough for me to slide through.

I couldn't get in fast enough. My search was finally over.

Behind me, the door was shut, the chains were rewound, and the lock clicked.

CHAPTER 12

The building had enough cracks and gaps inside, plus a hole in the sagging roof, so the room was dimly lit. Even so, it was hard to see much of anything, there were so many mounds of abandoned tools and equipment.

"Britt?" I called. Was she conscious? Had she been fed or given any water? "Britt," I called again, trying to find any sign of her amid all the discarded junk. But she wasn't there.

I sank to the floor, and a foreign stinging hit my eyes. Getting kidnapped to find Britt was one thing, but now I was just a random dude who'd voluntarily been locked in a shed.

Stupid. Stupid. Stupid.

The light faded. No doubt a cloud covering the sun for total symbolism. Then there was a scuffling sound. I jumped to my feet. Was I sharing this shed with a family of raccoons?

"Holt?"

My head snapped up. Had I hallucinated Brittany's voice?

"Britt?" I asked. Had I really lost my mind?

I still couldn't see her, and the light in the shed was getting darker. Glancing at the hole in the roof, I saw a pair of legs dangling into the room.

Hold on.

Was that...?

A figure dropped down through the roof, and there stood Brittany.

Let the record show I didn't faint at the sight of her. I sat down. Quickly. With no chair. Is that better than passing out?

"Holt!" Britt moved quickly to where I was sprawled on the floor, then hesitated. "Is that you?"

"Yeah." Did I sound angry? "Of course it's me."

"You're..." Britt paused, seeming to think. "Are you all right?"

Struggling to my feet was hard to do with my arms still bound. And I tried to do it without Britt's help. "Of course I'm all right." I definitely sounded angry. "Are you all right? You're the one who's been missing for days."

Britt ignored the question, instead pulling my face down to her eye level and analyzing it. Even in the low light, that scar by her eyebrow was obvious. Somehow I'd pictured this rescue mission going a little differently. So much for the kiss with fireworks.

"Did you hit your head?" she asked, still scrutinizing me.

"No," I said, batting her hands away from my face.

I hadn't. Right?

At least, I couldn't remember any head injuries.

"We need to make a plan," she said.

I brightened. "Yes. I've been thinking about that for days. Seattle's way too far away from Amelia's Haven. I can't actually live in Amelia's Haven because, well, vomit. But Carentorrie's only an hour away. I can get a job there, and we can see each other all the time—" I was interrupted by a sudden and monstrous yawn.

"Um." Brittany was biting her lip. Was she hiding a smile? "For right now, all I meant was a plan to get out of here alive."

"Oh." I'd kind of forgotten about that. There'd been a plan...What was it? I frowned, trying to remember my morning. Then it came to me. "I'm being tracked."

For the first time since seeing me, Britt looked relieved. "By the police?"

"Well...no." How did I explain? "I stole Chouzie's tracker and left a note for Juniper to check the coordinates."

"Uh-huh." The scar was back on her forehead.

"No, we're good. See?" I dug into my pockets—which wasn't easy to do with my arms bound. Instead of the tracker, all I came up with was my wallet and Darren's keys. "Um, it should be here." I rechecked my pockets in the vain hope it would magically appear. I frowned at Darren's keys. Hadn't they fallen into the lake?

Wait. The keys were in my hand, meaning the tracker had fallen into the water.

Awkward.

Clearing my throat, I met Brittany's eyes. "There might be one slight hiccup."

As I explained my failed plan, Brittany rifled through some of the junk in the shed. At one point she asked, "You got kidnapped on purpose?"

"Yes."

She shook her head. "That's the worst idea I've ever heard."

"Oh." I didn't trust myself to say anything else. My eyes were in danger of leaking—it must've been from all the dust in the shed.

Britt gave my arm a squeeze. "Sorry. That was rude. You've clearly been dealing with a lot of...stress."

What was that supposed to mean?

It was important to remember how glad and relieved I was Brittany was alive. I didn't need to be a sulky butt about her not loving my brilliant plan. It had worked, hadn't it? Or, it had sort of worked. Aside from the tracker part, which was sort of the whole point of the plan...

"Now, you need to stand very still." Britt was holding a rusted tool full of tiny sharp tines vaguely resembling a handsaw.

"I'm scared," I said, taking a step back.

"Don't worry," she said. "I got this."

"What is that? Where did you get it?"

Brittany took a deep breath. Next she set down the sharp thing and took a step toward me with her palms up. "Here. Sit down for me." She sheep-dogged me to a pile of junk below the gap in the roof. "Yup, right here in the light. Okay." Britt had a hand on my shoulder and was looking me straight in the eye. "I need you to relax. We're going to free your arms."

It's not that I thought she was about to torture me, but I still squirmed when Britt limped away to get the saw-thing. *Limped?*

"You're hurt?"

Britt brushed a strand of hair out of her face. "Not bad. Just a sprained ankle."

"Brittany!"

"I'm fine." She tried to laugh. "You're right. Stalking is a bad idea. I never would have, but it was Jeremy's..."

I nodded. "Sienna told me."

"Okay." Britt seemed relieved. "Anyway, you'd just fallen asleep when Scott left, and I followed. He picked someone up, then drove to a gravel road. I turned off my lights and went down the road."

What?

Brittany had driven down that logging road with her lights out? I was in the car!

"Scott's truck was idling a little ways down, so I pulled off the road where they couldn't see me. Scott got out, and the truck turned around and drove away. He just stood there waiting. Then Gina drove up. They got flashlights and started walking into the woods. So..."

Brittany bit her lip. "I decided to go after them. You were unrespon-sive, so I locked you in the car and went in the direction of their lights. Just when I'd gotten close enough to see them, Gina took a gun from her purse and shot Scott." Her voice trembled. "I was so surprised I screamed. Then Gina knew I was there. I tried to run away, but I couldn't see much in the dark. I tripped and fell bad. After that, I couldn't move fast enough, and Gina caught up with me." Brittany shook her head. "Maybe I should have tried harder, but she had a gun and a flashlight...I was just so scared."

I would have wrapped my arms around her, but since they were tied, I rested my head on her shoulder. "You did everything you could." My voice also trembled. "You have no idea how worried I was."

"Well"—Britt's lips quirked—"I have an idea." Before I could com-ment, she said, "Now, hold still." Brittany moved my arms into a ray of light. Next, she maneuvered the thing that wasn't quite a saw to the row of zip ties and began the careful process of freeing my arms.

It was terrifying. Would an accidental nick give me tetanus?

"Holt?"

"Hm?"

Britt was working on the last tie. "Did you hear me?"

She'd been talking?

"Uh, no."

The scar was back on her forehead. "Okay. Well, I was saying, after I'd wrapped my ankle, I searched for a way out."

"Makes sense," I said.

"Uh-huh." Again Brittany seemed amused, but I didn't know why. "The whole shed will topple over with a few more winters, but right now the roof was the weakest spot. I found the section with the worst sagging and piled the junk so I had a sort of ladder to reach it. Then

I got to work creating a hole and making it big enough to climb through."

"So resourceful," I muttered.

I was being shaken. "Hey, stay awake."

"Sure."

Brittany was down to the last couple of ties. "It took two days, but I got it done this morning. I was planning on stealing the boat the next time Gina returned. But this time..." Was Britt blushing? "This time, she came with you."

The final tie snapped off, and my arms were free. We'd still never kissed. Had barely touched. Yet, at that moment, I didn't try to kiss her. Instead, I wrapped my arms around her, crushing her to my chest. "I'm so glad you're alive."

Brittany wrapped her arms around me, and we stayed like that until Britt said, "Holt?" The sound was muffled through my shirt.

"Yeah?"

"I can't breathe."

I let go immediately. "Sorry."

"You're good. Let's go." She tugged at my arm. "Now."

Brittany insisted I climb out first. The roof wasn't very high. Still, it was a precarious climb. Britt directed exactly where each step should go on her ladder of rusty machinery. It made awful groaning sounds under my weight. "Will this hold?" I asked near the top of the pile.

"It should."

I wanted to point out I weighed a lot more than her, but I'd reached the roof and was beginning to climb through. It was a tight squeeze, and my shirt tore in the process, but I managed.

Finding a sturdy section of roof, I leaned down to watch Britt's progress. The tension on her face and the way she favored her right side showed her ankle was more of a problem than she'd admitted. When she got to the opening, I offered her a hand up.

I was the first to land on earth, and it was done rather awkward-ly—though nothing but my dignity was bruised. Brittany let me help lower her down, and soon we were both on solid ground.

Once we were both safe, I yawned for so long, black spots speckled my vision. Britt had a hand securely on my elbow, and again I had the annoying suspicion she was worried about me.

I shook her off. "I'm fine," I said.

"Help me walk" was all she said.

Oh. I was a jerk.

But even as I wrapped my arm around her and supported her bad side on the walk to the water, I had the suspicion Britt was doing this for my benefit. At the dock, Gina's boat was long gone, but the water was still a better escape route than attempting to climb the rocks surrounding us.

From what I remembered of the boat ride, this section of the lake was wild and unpopulated. One of us could try swimming out and raising the alert of a passing boat, but Britt had a sprained ankle and hadn't been given regular meals. When I suggested swimming out, Britt didn't even pause before shooting that idea down.

"Why not?" I asked. Britt made a face that was part smile and part grimace before gesturing at my general appearance. *Why were people doing that?*

I was about to argue when there was a hum of an approaching mo-tor. I would have stayed staring at the shoreline, but Brittany grabbed my arm and dragged me behind a tree. Gina's speedboat appeared. She didn't go to the dock. Instead, she cut the engine and floated by the far side of the rocks. She stayed there, never bothering to glance toward land. What was she doing?

Resting my head against the tree, I tried to remember to stay awake. Whatever guilt had kept me awake for days had vanished since finding Britt alive. Even being within eyesight of a kidnapping murderer with a gun was doing little to keep me alert.

Fingers dug into my skin, and I was too tired to cry out. When I raised an eyebrow at Britt, she whispered, "Just a little longer."

Right. Danger and all that. Squinting at Gina, I tried to feel scared or threatened or something that would keep me from going fetal on the ground.

After an unbearable amount of time, where I caught myself dozing more than once, Gina's posture relaxed. She turned the boat on and headed for the exit. My eyes squeezed shut with a yawn, so I missed the moment she returned with a police boat on her tail. There was a second exit I hadn't noticed. It was narrower than the first, but Gina steered expertly toward it, only to be blocked in by a second police boat. Running out of options, she steered to the shore and leapt onto the dock without tying off the boat, then sprinted off. But where could she go? Gina was trapped, unless this was actually the Batcave, with a maze of underground escape routes.

The police boats were close behind. Both boats stopped by the dock, but the officers hesitated at the rickety boards and made it across one at a time. They did move quickly, and in under a minute there were quite a lot of uniforms onshore.

Spotting The Local Sheriff in the crowd of unknowns, Britt and I left our hideout. We moved slowly with our hands held high. As soon as we were spotted, a myriad of instructions were given—an inconvenient time to have trouble concentrating. Brittany was practically dragged away from me, though she kept saying we were together. At some point in the chaos, I was instructed to lie down in the dirt and was patted down for weapons. At least I wasn't being handcuffed, and the ground was surprisingly comfortable.

"You're an idiot!"

Juniper?

I rolled to my side, and sure enough, there was my baby sister with her arms crossed and hip popped. I groaned and got to my feet with the help of Juniper and The Local Sheriff.

"Let's get you to the boat while we apprehend the suspect." The sheriff still looked grim, but this time it wasn't directed at me.

On the other hand, Juniper directed all her anger at me. "What would compel you to steal a dog tracker to lure a murderer?"

I froze. "So it worked?" I managed not to yawn. "It fell into the water."

Juniper rolled her eyes. "Yeah, genius. The tracker's waterproof. Remember? Dogs have a penchant for swimming."

Right. She'd bought the super-duper tracker with its own satellite.

"Don't smile," Juniper said, even as she helped me into the police boat. "This was an awful idea."

"So I've heard," I said.

That threw Juniper off her game. She pursed her lips and glared.

"Lighten up," I said. "It worked, didn't it? What are you going to do? Tell Mom?"

"Don't tempt me." She huffed.

The Local Sheriff led us to the upper deck, where Brittany sat waiting. My heart tightened. It was like I was seeing her for the first time. Her days of captivity showed on her face, but it didn't matter. She would remain the most dazzling woman in the world after a month with the flu.

Without overthinking it, I sat right beside her and wrapped an arm around her. "Happy Independence Day," I said.

Brittany snuggled closer. "Happy Fourth."

This was perfect. Tonight we'd go to Coeur d'Alene and watch the city's fireworks, just like we'd planned...if her mom let us.

The Local Sheriff ruined the moment by asking Brittany, "Did you see who killed Scott?"

"I know what happened," I murmured, resting my head on top of Britt's.

CHAPTER 13

Fingers were pressing into my wrist, and my arm was raised. I let out a sigh and shifted. The pressure on my wrist lessened, and my arm was placed gently on my stomach.

When I peeked an eye open, it was to find Britt leaning over me. Her color was better, and she'd freshened up. Catching the movement, Brittany's eyes locked with mine. As if in slow motion, I sat up and pulled Britt onto my lap. We gave each other one final look before our eyes closed, and we kissed—for a while.

"Do you want lemonade?" Juniper called.

Brittany tumbled off my lap to sit beside me a moment too late.

"Holt Jacobs," Juniper said, way too excited.

"What?"

Juniper giggled. "Do you want lemonade?"

I rubbed at my eyes. I wasn't sure what time it was, but I knew what I needed. "Can I get some coffee?"

"Sure thing, sleepyhead." Juniper left, and only then did I really notice I was on The Hive's uncomfortable sofa. Wasn't I on a boat? How had I gotten here?

I was going to ask when Brittany faced me. "Do you remember your plan for the future?"

That took me a second. If anything, the last few days resembled a fever dream instead of reality. "Carentorrie?" I asked.

Britt nodded, but beyond that, I couldn't tell if she liked the idea or would prefer I start a colony on Mars. Why didn't she say anything?

"Was that...okay?"

She was surprised. "You meant it?"

I thought momentarily about how cold and empty life in Seattle would be without her. "I haven't had my coffee yet," I said with a lazy smile. "But yeah. I meant it."

"Okay." Britt's eyes were soft. "You know, I'd been planning on moving away with Jeremy after the wedding. But with his death and everything going on with my family, I stayed put. But now I'm more than ready for a fresh start. So"—she tucked invisible strands of hair behind her ear—"I was thinking Seattle."

If any other almost girlfriend had told me this, I would have started freaking out. But since it was Britt, a jaw-splitting grin covered my face. "Yeah?"

"Yeah."

We were mid-kiss when Juniper returned with my coffee and two lemonades. I couldn't hide my happiness from Juniper, but I wasn't ready to tell her why. Juniper handed us our drinks with a smirk.

I laced the fingers of my free hand with Brittany's. "Are we still watching the fireworks tonight?"

"Holt..." Britt bit her lip.

Was it her ankle?

"Are you all right?"

Had I been banished?

"Did your mom disinvite me?"

Before Britt could answer, Juniper cut in. "Her mom hates you! Like, I thought Darren was exaggerating when he said she called the cops on you. But no. She blames you for everything."

"I mean..." Britt was red-faced. "That's not quite accurate...It's, uh..."

Oh. Right.

After clearing my throat, I decided to change the subject. "Were they able to catch Gina?"

"Yeah, they got her." Juniper tossed her hair back. "Jude also tracked down Scott's friends, and they gave up Mr. Camarata."

"How did Jude do that?"

"Oh, you know." Juniper shrugged. "A little of this and a little of that."

Um...what?

"I literally don't know," I said. "That's why I asked." When Juniper remained quiet, I asked, "Remind me what Jude's job is?"

"Um..." Juniper nibbled on a fingernail. "He works for the government."

Wait. Wasn't that code for spy? Was Jude actually the American James Bond?

Brittany rested a hand on my knee. "Sheriff Misty's been wanting to take your statement"—her mouth quirked—"but you've been unresponsive every time she's been by."

After taking a long gulp of coffee, I asked a simple question. "What time is it?"

Britt said, "It's a little after two."

So I'd had a decent nap.

Juniper snorted. "It's after two on July fifth."

I narrowed my eyes. "But that would mean I was asleep for—"

"Over twenty-four hours?" Juniper cut in. "Yes. Yes, you were."

Britt gave my knee a squeeze. "Guess why I was checking your pulse."

I looked from one to the other, expecting them to break any second and start laughing. They didn't.

"Here." Britt handed me her phone. "Look at the date."

Okay, so there's a chance they were telling the truth, and I'd literally slept the day away.

"That's why we can't watch the fireworks," Britt said. "You weren't awake for them."

Wait. Britt was missing for our third date, and I'd slept through the fourth?

"You know," I said, grinning, "we have the absolute worst dates."

"Agreed," Britt said.

We were about to kiss again, but Juniper's "Gross!" stopped us.

I tried to run a hand through my hair, but my fingers didn't slide through the way they normally did. Frowning, I asked, "How did I end up here? Last thing I remember was on the boat."

Juniper's eyes lit up with merriment. She was instantly making a spot for herself, sandwiching me in between the two of them. "Oh, let's see," she said, swiping at her phone. "Well, here's you on the drive back." In the shot, I was nothing but hair, arms, and legs sprawled across the back seat of my car. Juniper tapped the screen. "And this is you getting to the car." This image was of Darren carrying me in a fireman's hold while my arms, head, and hair were limp, rag-dolled by gravity. "Then here you are," Juniper continued, pulling up a new image, "on the boat."

I took the phone in my hands and grinned. I was clearly down for the count, still holding on to Britt and, even asleep, smiling like a lion who'd just been named king of the jungle. Wait. What was that...? Frowning, I zoomed in. What was that on my face? Was that supposed to be facial hair? With a look like that, it's a wonder people hadn't been calling me Oscar the Grouch. My frown deepened as I zoomed in even closer. Was that a stain on my shirt? On my white golf polo shirt?

Gasping, I tossed the phone at Juniper and jumped off the couch to face them. I needed to get some distance between us. My mouth opened and closed, my mind racing too fast to form words.

"Is something wrong?" Juniper was enjoying this a little too much.

"The fifth...It's...but you said it's the fifth."

"Yes, Holt." Britt's whole demeanor was of a first responder dealing with a meltdown, but the quirk of her lips gave her away. She was enjoying this as much as Juniper.

"I showered and dressed the day of the stakeout. That was the first."

They nodded.

"Today's the fifth," I repeated. "I...I haven't showered or shaved or—" I clasped a hand over my mouth, suddenly nauseated. "I haven't brushed my teeth in days."

"Mm-hmm," Juniper managed through laughter so hard her eyes were filling with tears. She'd better not be filming this.

Brittany stood up slowly with arms raised like she was approaching a panicked horse. "You were under a lot of stress."

The fact the scar by her eyebrow wasn't visible showed she wasn't actually worried, which made it so much worse. Britt moved closer. "Why don't you sit down and take some deep breaths. It's okay. You're in a safe place."

For a moment I considered her words, weighing them against all the sweaty walks, the food stains, the dirt, and the large tear from climbing through a shed's roof. Then Britt took one step closer, and my head snapped up. I nearly tripped over my own feet in my haste to escape from her.

"You...you kissed..." I gestured toward Juniper's phone. "You kissed that? What's wrong with you?" I had to stop talking as another wave of nausea hit. I glared at her and began backing toward the stairs and the shower.

Why was no one taking this seriously? Britt had kissed (and I mean really kissed) a man who hadn't brushed his teeth in days. I gagged. Britt was instantly by my side, but I shook her off. "I don't know about this." I gestured between us. "The kiss...that kiss...How can a relationship make it when the first kiss was so...abhorrent?"

Juniper burst into a new bout of laughter. "Even Chouzie wouldn't go near you."

Britt gave my sister a withering glare I'd never seen before. "Not helping," she said.

For maybe half a second, Juniper looked remorseful. Britt deserved a medal.

As for me, I was going to shower. And burn my clothes. And bleach my mouth. And fix the rat's nest on my face and head—even if I had to go bald for the second time this year.

"Are you really breaking up over this?" Juniper asked.

I looked between the two of them, and they were still amused.

"Five days!" I yelled.

"I hope you guys can work it out," Juniper called as I trudged to the stairs. "While you were sleeping, we made plans for a weekend away. It'll be awkward if you guys aren't together."

"And I was moving to Seattle," Britt added.

I shuddered.

Great. Just great.

———◆◇◆———

What do a bad glass of wine, a corkscrew, and a murdered ex-girl-friend have in common? Read Holt's next mystery *A Not So Rosy Vintage* to find out.

Ready for a Holt Jacobs snack-sized mystery? Sign up for my newsletter at *lilystirling.com* and receive a copy of *Holt Jacobs & The Mystery Of The Missing Sunglasses,* plus delightful every-other-week emails.

MAGNIFICENT!

Way to earn your super-sleuth badge for completing Holt Jacobs's second book! I hope you enjoyed his Idaho adventure.

My mom's one complaint about this book is how many jokes Holt makes at Idaho's expense.

But speaking as someone whose birth certificate says *Idaho* on it, I can confidently state there aren't positive representations of Idaho in fiction or nonfiction. At best, you get something neutral like, "Have you tried their potatoes?"

Are there good things about Idaho? Absolutely. Is Holt Jacobs the person to give a groundbreaking and nuanced view of Idaho? Nope.

Maybe I need a disclaimer.

The views and opinions expressed in this book are those of Holt Jacobs and do not necessarily reflect the views or positions of the author, Lily Stirling.

Happy Mom?

What did you think of the book? Should Holt have given a monologue at the end about how beautiful the lake and the trees were?

Whatever you thought, it would be super helpful to me and potential readers if you left a review.

Do you have a favorite part?

One paragraph I always smile at is, *'Besides chips and drinks, I ended up buying sandwiches from the deli section. They weren't exactly appe-*

tizing, but definitely less questionable than the sushi.' I believe everyone who's ever traveled has had to make a 'lesser of two evils' decision when it comes to eating on the road. Also, my dad thought up the *sushi* bit, and I love that we collaborated.

I hope to see you for Holt's next mystery, *A Not So Rosy Vintage*. Seriously, I am so excited about this murder mystery at a Washington winery—it might secretly be my favorite.

If you want to hang out some more, join my newsletter at *lilystirling.com*. You'll get every-other-week updates, plus Holt's snack-sized story, *Holt Jacobs & The Mystery Of The Missing Sunglasses.*

Thanks for reading!

~ Lily Stirling

P.S. If you get the chance to see Coeur d'Alene's Fourth of July fireworks, do yourself a favor and be one of the fancy people watching from a boat...it'll save you the hassle of being stuck in traffic on the way home.

ABOUT THE AUTHOR

Lily Stirling is the writer and creator of the Holt Jacob Mystery series.

She has spent a quarter of a century living in the Pacific Northwest. Lily was born in Idaho, but her family moved to Washington around the time she could read chapter books.

Mysteries have always delighted her, from listening to *The Hardy Boys* on car trips to watching episodes of *Psych*.

As for sarcastic families, when she's not writing about one, she's living in one.

HOLT JACOBS MYSTERY SERIES

A Not So Shocking Murder
A Not So Rustic Retreat

ACKNOWLEDGEMENTS

Here's the thing, this book could have an ugly duckling to beautiful swan transformation montage—think *Princess Diaries* when the stylists are snapping Anne Hathaway's glasses in half and straightening her hair.

My production team were the gifted artists and technicians who helped get my book to this point. Thank you all so much. I'm so glad each one of you was involved with my book.

Production Team:

Developmental Editor ~ Kristen Weber

Copyeditor ~ Penina Lopez

Proofreader ~ Elaini Caruso

Cover Designer ~ Mariah Sinclair

<hr />

Mom and Dad, thank you for always being available to listen as I monologue about Holt Jacobs, writing, and publishing—plus being great parents in other aspects of my life. You're both so amazing.

Thanks to my siblings and in-laws. You're all so creative and talented. Thank you for setting such wonderful examples of the hard work and discipline it takes to finish creative projects.

Huge thanks to my mom's friend, Jenny, for reading a draft and loving Holt's friend, Darren.

Finally, thank *you* for taking the time to read my book and making it through the acknowledgments. I hope you love Holt Jacobs and his family as much as I do.

Thanks again!

~ *Lily Stirling*